Chapter 1 – "Sorry we're closed"

Nineteen Ninety something

Don was pissed off.

It was gone midnight on a Friday night, and he was stuck at work. His wife Sarah was out partying, and he envied her. Her best friend Kim had invited her to a hen night, and she was pleased to be able to have a girl's night out. It had been ages since the last one. He had dropped her off at Kim's before coming to work and had agreed to pick her up in the morning.

Meanwhile, he was working on his own and he'd had enough.

He was the owner of "View-it videos", a business which he'd inherited from his father who had died six months before of a heart attack right on the spot that he was now working. It hadn't taken him long to realise that keeping a record of a large stock of videos would be far easier on a computer, and he had spent the best part of the week entering all the titles into the newly acquired IBM PC. He was nearly finished and was hoping to get away soon so he could get a decent night's sleep before picking Sarah up and coming back to work again.

Around forty minutes later he returned the last of the videos to the shelf while backing up the work he had done on the computer. If the backup didn't take long, he might just get a drink in. He looked at his watch and noticed that it had stopped at 1:03. Is it really that late he thought checking the clock on the wall? 12:40. Bloody watch stopped hours ago. It was new – a present from Sarah. He hoped she'd kept the receipt so he could take it back. The computer beeped and he forgot his watch and grabbed the disk from the drive. He switched off the PC and went into the storeroom to put the disk into the safe.

A large man walked into the video shop and locked the door behind him. He heard movement at the back of the shop and headed towards it.

Spinning a dial of the safe he heaved a sigh of relief. It had been a long and painful task but at last it was done.

He heard someone come in and shouted out, 'sorry we're closed'.

He turned the light off in the storeroom and went to see his customer. All he got was a split-second glimpse of a fist coming towards him. He hit the ground hard, smashing his watch on the floor and sending it sliding across the room. He looked up blinking, trying to see who his attacker was but the man struck again, lashing out with his foot, shattering a couple of Don's ribs. He felt himself being lifted off the ground and panic set in as two large hands encircled his throat and began to squeeze. His protests stopped about twenty seconds later but the man didn't let go for a couple of minutes.

He dragged the limp body to the back of the storeroom, covered it with an old sheet and switched off the lights in the front of the shop. He was about to leave when he noticed the security camera. It didn't take long to find the video player. He wound the tape back a couple of minutes and watched himself enter the shop. Winding back again he pressed record to wipe over the short period in which he was there. He left by the emergency exit at the back of the storeroom. Nobody saw him.

ZAK

Jason Diggle

Chapter 2 – "A Robbery"

Zak walked through the deserted streets keeping to the shadows despite the overcast night. There was only a quarter moon and most of that was shrouded in cloud. A light rain began to fall, and he swore under his breath.

He turned into the high street and carried on up past the "Sheep's Head" which had closed several hours earlier. The rank smell of beer turned his stomach and he quickened his pace. He had staggered out of that particular pub on a number of occasions and he smiled as he remembered how, on the last night of his famous visit he had attempted to leave with the "last orders" bell, ringing it on the way to help clear a path. This had resulted in the bell being kept chained to the bar and him nearly being barred from the pub. For the following week whenever the bell rang, a hearty cheer let rip from around the bar. It was an incident that wasn't forgotten in a hurry. This prank was topped a couple of months later however when the bell was actually stolen complete with chain, and the landlord was sent a postcard from Barbados with a photo of the bell wearing a large pair of sunglasses, sitting on a sunbed proclaiming "Wish you were here".

Zak approached the top of the hill, chuckling to himself as he recalled past memories of his drinking days at the pub. He glanced around to check he was still alone and was pleased to see the streets deserted. The rain had picked up and he had to squint to keep the water from his eyes. Who else would be mad enough to be out on a night like this he thought? He hurried on, his mind now on the job at hand. When the video shop came into sight he reached into his pocket and took out a small bunch of tools. He took another quick glance around before starting on the lock. It took him less than thirty seconds to get the door open.

He strolled into the shop giving a little wave to the security camera on the way in. On previous occasions he had dropped his trousers for such cameras, but the chilly night had put him off that idea. He made his way past the rows of videos heading for the safe. Rental shops such as these weren't huge money spinners but if he was lucky, he might get a couple of thousand.

The safe was in a dark storeroom at the back of the shop. He had seen the manager of the shop taking the money from the till into the storeroom on several occasions while he was browsing in the new release section. He crouched down by the safe and flicked a small penlight torch on. It gave him just enough light for the job. He pulled on the handle of the safe. Always worth a try he mused, not really surprised when it didn't open. Zak removed a small device from inside his jacket pocket. It operated in the same way as a stethoscope but had a mini amplifier built in. One end had a sucker on it which he stuck to the safe above the dial.

A few minutes later he had the door open. He grabbed the piles of notes and put them inside his jacket with the tools. He never carried a bag as he thought it was too conspicuous. He always associated it with that cartoon character who carried a bag with "Swag" stamped across it in big black letters. What was his name? He couldn't remember. He swung the safe door shut and made his way back through the shop, checking he hadn't left anything behind. Satisfied he blew a kiss to the camera and went back out.

The street was still quiet, and Zak spent about twenty seconds locking the door behind him. It was an operation which he always did if possible. Nobody would notice the break in until the shop opened in the morning. He pictured the manager trying to explain to the police that there had been a break in but there was no evidence except his performances on the security camera.

He pulled his jacket collar up to shield the rain and headed back to the centre of town, stopping just once to remove the latex mask he was wearing.

****

Marty was sleeping rough again. He had been out of work for nearly two years now and the money had run out. He couldn't afford to drink as well as have a roof over his head and just lately the drink seemed far more important. He had put his head down an hour earlier on a park bench, but the rain had woken him. As it got heavier, he struggled to his feet and clutching his half full bottle of whisky took a drunken walk into town. He always liked to think of the bottle as half full, never half empty. He chuckled aloud at the thought of this and took another swig.

The bottle was about a quarter full by the time he reached the first shop and his sway was becoming far more prominent. He collapsed in the shop doorway which was sheltered from most of the rain and fell asleep.

He was woken a bit later by the sound of footsteps. He glanced up and saw a man coming his way. The man stopped for a brief moment and took his face off. Marty rubbed his eyes. He'd definitely had too much tonight. He looked again and saw the man tuck his face into his bulging pocket. That pocket looked like it may contain money. The man started walking down the road towards him again. He grabbed his bottle and took a large swig. Don't want to waste too much he thought. If he'd been sober, he would never have contemplated his next actions, but the drink had started doing the talking long ago.

As Zak walked past the doorway, the drunken tramp staggered out and brought the bottle crashing down on his victim's head. Zak crashed to the floor unconscious and Marty gave a triumphant shout. He had hoped to make a few pounds out of his attack but had never expected anything like this. He counted the money. There was over fifteen hundred pounds. Marty grabbed the money and disappeared as fast as his drunken state would allow. As he wove down the street, he tucked the money away in various items of clothing. Things were definitely looking up.

Zak was unfortunate enough to be found by a policeman. PC Gibbons was doing his regular beat through the town centre at 04.00 am when he discovered the body sprawled outside of C & A. He checked Zak's pulse and found that he was still alive. Noticing a cut on the head he called for an ambulance on his radio. As he waited, he checked the man's pockets for identification and found a grubby driving licence in his wallet. Zak McDonald. He wrote down the name and address and noted the time. As he placed the wallet back, he saw the latex mask and jumped back in shock, realising a second or two later what it was. He was glad he was on his own. He could just imagine the stick he would have got from his workmates if they had seen him jump like that. He examined the mask and frowned. Strange item to carry around he thought. He went through all of Zak's pockets and turned out the tools and the 'safe cracker'. The policeman gave a broad grin. Caught in the act he thought. Go to jail. Do not collect any money whatsoever!

The ambulance arrived and carried Zak off to the hospital. Gibbons accompanied him. He wanted to be the first to talk to him when he came around.

Chapter 3 – "Dead?"

Sarah wasn't feeling her best. The party had been good at the time, but she was beginning to regret having too much to drink. She remembered downing about half a pint of lager in one go, not much by a lot of people's standards but after a bottle of wine and two shots, the lager just about tipped her past consciousness. When she woke up, her friend Kim had forced to drink two cups of very strong black coffee which didn't stay down for very long. She declined breakfast in favour of a couple of aspirin.

Kim was fine. She had also had a fair amount to drink, but she was used to drinking larger quantities than Sarah. She was tucking greedily into a fried breakfast which wasn't helping Sarah's stomach at all.

'So, when's Don picking you up?' asked Kim between mouthfuls.

'He said he'd be here no later than eleven' said Sarah wincing at the pain in her head. 'What time is it now?'

'Quarter past, he's late. Perhaps he had a few too many as well'.

'No. He was working late. And he had the car. He wouldn't go over the limit while he was driving' said Sarah. 'Shit, I wish I could shift this bloody headache. How come you're OK?'

'Lucky I guess' said Kim grinning. 'I don't drink beer in large quantities like you'.

'I didn't have much' protested Sarah. 'It didn't go very well with the wine that's all'.

Kim laughed as she took the empty plate to the sink.

'I hope you've cleaned my bathroom properly', she said. 'If I find the remains of any carrots in the sink, you're dead'.

Sarah groaned. 'Can I use your phone?' she said. 'I'll give Don a ring - see where he's got to'.

She dialled the number and let it ring.

'Come on Don, pick it up' she mumbled. She put it down after the twelfth ring. 'Must be on his way'. she called out. 'I'll get my things ready'.

At twelve o'clock Sarah was getting impatient. She had tried phoning home again and even tried the shop but to no avail.

'Where the hell is he?' she remarked for the fourth time. 'He's over an hour late. He should have opened the shop by now'.

'Come on, I'll take you home' said Kim. 'If he shows up here later, I'll tell him you ran off with a nineteen-year old toy-boy last night'.

'Tell him it was twins' said Sarah with a glint in her eye. 'Thanks'. She grabbed her overnight bag. 'Can you run by the shop first? Perhaps he just forgot'.

'OK, let's go'.

****

They arrived at the shop to find it swarming with police and cameramen. They had put up tape around the area and were trying hard to keep the news crews back.

Sarah leapt out of the car and headed straight for the shop. She lifted the tape and a policeman stopped her.

'Sorry madam, you can't go in there' he said.

'It's my shop' she yelled, trying to be heard over all the commotion. 'What's going on?'.

The cameras suddenly turned on her as someone overheard what she had said. She squinted against the flashbulbs and her headache reached an all-time high.

'Can I take your name please madam?' The policeman was trying hard to ignore the swarming media. Sarah told him her name and he signalled to an officer who had just left the shop.

'This is the wife' he said quietly. 'She's just arrived'. The policeman nodded and led her under the tape and into the shop. Kim had parked the car and was scrambling after her, trying to get past another burly policeman. Sarah stopped.

'She's with me' she said going back towards Kim. The officer nodded and the policeman let her through.

The shop had been taken over by police and they appeared to be hording around the stockroom. Sarah and Kim were led to one side and they sat down while the news was broken to them.

'Dead?' whispered Sarah in shock, visibly paling. 'Are you sure?'.

She realised it was a silly question, but her head was spinning, and she wasn't thinking straight.

'I'm afraid so madam' said the officer gently.

'How?' asked Sarah looking up at him in distress. 'How did he die?'

'We don't have all the details yet madam, but we believe he was strangled'.

The officer seemed to go in and out of focus and she had a crazy moment where she thought she might be dreaming.

'You mean he was murdered?' she cried, her voice going up an octave. 'Is that what you're saying? - That my husband was murdered?'

'Well we don't know all the details yet' said the policeman awkwardly. 'We're still investigating at this stage. We will know for sure later when the body has been examined'.

'I want to see him' said Sarah. 'I have to see him to believe it'.

'Are you sure you want to?' said Kim soothingly. 'I mean, do you think you are ready to see him?'.

'I must see him' she said more firmly.

The officer led Sarah to the storeroom and stopped outside.

'Ready?' he said.

Sarah nodded, took a deep breath and walked in. Her heart missed a beat when she saw him. He was laid under a white sheet in the middle of the storeroom. There was dried blood on his nose, and his neck was swollen and bruised all the way round. His eyes were open and stared vacantly towards her.

She gasped and turned away sobbing nearly knocking over the coroner who had just arrived. She reached her chair just before she fainted.

Chapter 4 – "This town. Is coming like a ghost town…"

'Looks like he is coming around'.

'About time to' grumbled Gibbons, getting up and stretching. 'My legs are beginning to fall asleep. How soon will I be able to question him?'

'Not for a while, he will be a bit drowsy at first'. The nurse looked closely at Zak. He had begun mumbling something sleepily and his eyelids were flickering erratically. The nurse put her ear closer to his mouth but couldn't make out what he was trying to say. After a couple of seconds, he relaxed again and dozed softly. Gibbons sighed impatiently.

'Is there anywhere I can get a drink?' he asked her.

'Down the hall, first right' said the nurse without looking at him. She turned and headed for the door with the policeman close behind her. 'Do you really have to hang around here all day? Haven't you got better things to do with your time?'. She was getting fed up with him watching her every move. He seemed to be paying more attention to her than the man he had brought in.

'Just doing my job' he said, his eyes admiring her long legs as he trotted behind her. 'Besides, it beats pounding the streets in this weather. Bloody rain hasn't let up in hours. This way is it?' She had stopped at the adjoining corridor.

'Yes. Just by the lift'. She hurried on up the corridor leaving him standing there, feeling his eyes burning into the back of her.

'Bloody pervert', she mumbled under her breath. She glanced back as she turned a corner and saw him duck into the hospital cafe.

****

Zak was drifting. His mind kept racing through different points in his life as he lay in his unconscious slumber. He was twenty–five, driving home from a party with his wife Mary, sleeping silently beside him. The radio was playing one of his favourite songs - Imagine, by John Lennon and he sang softly.

The party had been a bit of a disaster. It had been one of Mary's work colleagues who had invited them, and Zak hadn't known anybody. To pass the time he had had more to drink than he had intended too, and he feared that he might be over the limit. Mary had offered to drive but she had drunk just as much as him and wasn't feeling too good. He was pleased that she had fallen asleep so easily. It would make the journey less painful for her. The car came to an intersection and she stirred as he slowed down.

'Are we nearly there?' she asked sleepily.

'Not far honey' he replied. 'Go back to sleep, I'll wake you when we get there'.

She mumbled and settled down again as Zak pulled out onto the main road.

He was only four miles from home, singing along to Bryan Ferry when the front tyre blew. He wrestled hopelessly with the steering wheel and Mary awoke with a start. Before she could say anything, the car started to slide…..

…..The dodgem was sliding sideways and he shrieked with delight. He was fifteen, at the fairground with his best friend Ben Andrews, and couldn't remember a better day since the school had caught fire and they were all sent home for the afternoon. His dodgem was being pursued by Ben and another guy he didn't even know. He spun his car around in a tight circle to avoid them catching him, but someone else smashed him from the rear side. As he whirled around again, he saw that Ben had spun his wheel around and his dodgem was cruising around backwards with Ben looking over his shoulder to see where he was going. Zak fell about laughing as the backward dodgem went into a three-way crash with a couple of girls he'd been eyeing up earlier. The owner of the dodgems was not looking amused and he started gabbling into the microphone in his sales pitch voice.

'Keep the cars moving - one way round the track. Dodgems the name of the game. Lots of fun can be had riding the fabulous dodgem cars. Only one pound per car'.

His voice was wasted on the manic drivers. As far as they were concerned the only way to have fun was try and obliterate every other car on the track.

As the night wore on, Zak and Ben went on all the rides from the big wheel to the funhouse to the waltza, the ride that always guaranteed a thrill but more often than not, led to a "dicky stomach" as Ben put it. They staggered off barely able to stand up, then went straight on to the gravity wheel. They tried to win on the darts and the coconuts, spent a fortune on the arcade games and ended up back at the dodgems for a last attempt to annoy the man in charge.

It was eleven o'clock when they finally left the bright lights and music of the funfair. Some of the stalls had begun to close and Zak had promised to be home by eleven thirty.

'We'll have to come back before the fair moves on' said Ben enthusiastically. 'I've got a bit of cash left. How about Saturday? It's the last night. It's always good on the last night'.

'Sounds good to me. I'll have to try and get some money first. I'm skint after tonight. It was well worth it though'. Zak stifled a yawn. 'Let's take a shortcut through the graveyard, I'm knackered. We'll be home in no time'.

'You must be joking. You wouldn't catch me dead in there this time of night'.

'Not scared of a few corpses, are you?' said Zak mockingly. 'Come on, we'll be through it in a matter of minutes'. Zak hopped over the low wall and into the graveyard. Ben was a bit unsure but followed Zak anyway.

'You have to make sure you don't tread on any graves' said Zak in a low eerie voice. 'The natives get restless if you walk on them'.

Ben tensed up even more. He didn't like the graveyard in the daytime let alone this time of night. His older brother used to tell him ghost stories when he was younger, and this particular graveyard was always the subject of his spooky tales.

Zak started to sing an old hit by the Specials. 'This town. Is coming like a ghost town…'.

'Leave it out' said Ben picking up his pace. Let's get out of here'.

They walked on, Zak taunting Ben all the way. As they approached the old church in the middle of the graveyard Zak stopped suddenly.

'What was that?' he said looking behind him.

'Ha ha, very good' said Ben still walking. He was getting fed up with Zak. He'd been feeling very uneasy since they had come over the wall.

'No, listen' said Zak 'I'm sure I heard something'. He tilted his head in a listening gesture and cupped a hand over one ear. Ben grabbed him by the arm and started dragging him away.

'No honest' said Zak shaking him off. 'I swear I heard a sound, a kind of moaning'.

'The only person moaning around here is me' said Ben angrily. 'Now let's get out of here quick. You know how I feel about this place'.

They started walking again, Zak turning around occasionally and scanning the area behind them. Suddenly a thick mist started to emerge over them, restricting their view to a few feet. Now Zak was beginning to get worried.

'Sod this' he said. 'I can't see a bloody thing. Whose idea was this?'

'I wonder' said Ben sarcastically as he trudged on. 'Look, there's the streetlamp'. The light was at the entrance to the graveyard and it shone dimly through the fog. 'We're nearly there. This is definitely the last time you…..'. He screamed abruptly, making Zak jump, and fell over - rolling down a small embankment and out of Zak's view.

'Ben?' cried Zak. 'What happened? Are you alright?'

Zak's heart had started hammering and panic was beginning to set in.

'Where the hell are you?'

Then he heard it again. It was a low moaning sound just behind him. He spun round and saw a crouched figure scurrying off through the dark mist. Suddenly something struck him on the back of his head, and he fell and rolled down the hill. He stopped with a thud against a body and screamed. Realising it was Ben he jumped up and turned around to see who had hit him. The attacker switched on a bright light and shone it down directly onto Bens' body. Zak looked at Ben. His head was missing.

****

Zak woke with a scream and sat bolt upright in the hospital bed. Gibbons screamed louder in shock and jumped up, spilling his newly acquired coffee down the front of his uniform. It took Zak a few seconds to realise that his memories had turned into nightmares, and it was a few moments more before he took in his unfamiliar surroundings. The next thing that he noticed was that his head was pounding, which reminded him of the dream again. He realised he was in a hospital ward with a policeman, who was wiping stains out of his trousers and cursing.

A nurse rushed in.

'What happened?' she asked staring at the policeman's antics.

'Bloody idiot scared the living daylights out of me. Woke up screaming he did'. He turned to Zak. 'I could have you arrested for disturbing the peace'.

The nurse suppressed a smile and went over to Zak.

'How are you feeling?' she asked him as he settled back down onto the bed groaning.

'I've felt better' said Zak. 'What happened? Why am I here?'

His mind was racing trying to recall the events of the previous night. He remembered the robbery and walking home but everything else was a blank. There was a policeman with him so things must have gone wrong somehow.

'Don't worry' said the nurse kindly. 'It'll all come back to you eventually. You've had a knock on the head. I expect Mr Gibbons here will give you all the details. He bought you in late last night'.

Gibbons had given up trying to mop up all the coffee stains with his handkerchief, realising he was just spreading it further around.

'Can you tell me where the men's room is' he said. 'If I don't shift this coffee quick, I'll never get it out'.

'Opposite the coffee machine' said the nurse with a grin. She wasn't looking at Gibbons. She knew she would laugh at him if she did.

Gibbons strolled out, trying his best to cover the embarrassing stain that was spreading on his crotch. When he was out of earshot she sat down laughing. Even Zak managed a smile.

'And I thought I had problems' he said grinning. 'How bad is my head?'

The nurse recovered her composure. 'You'll live' she said. 'You got hit hard enough to knock you out but there's no permanent damage. We didn't even get a chance to attack you with a needle and thread'.

'How long have I been out?'

'About five hours, you were brought to us about four o'clock this morning. It's nine fifteen now. Are you hungry?'

'Hungry enough to manage some breakfast' said Zak stretching. 'Is hospital food really as bad as people say it is?'

'Worse' she replied with a whisper. 'But you didn't hear that from me'.

Zak smiled after her as she went to get him some breakfast. He wondered where his jacket had gone. He could see his clothes in a neat pile beside the bed, but his jacket wasn't with them. If the cop had it then he was in trouble. Might be worth getting out quick before he came back. He got out of bed and attempted to dress himself but became very lightheaded. He jumped back into bed with his damp jeans on and lay back to recover from his giddy spell.

Gibbons sauntered back in. He'd managed to remove the coffee stain but a large wet patched remained on the front of his trousers which looked far worse than the stain ever could of.

'Right then. I hope you're ready for a chat now Mr McDonald. I've been waiting here most of the night for you to come around and I'm in no mood to wait any longer'.

'What do you need to know?' asked Zak slowly. He had to think fast. If the cop knew his name, he must have searched him to find out.

'Can you tell me what you were doing about two o'clock this morning in the town centre carrying these items?'. He dumped Zak's tools on the bed and looked accusingly at him.

'You must be mistaken. These aren't mine'. Zak was thinking fast. Gibbons hadn't mentioned the money so there was a good chance it wasn't there when he was found. If he was lucky there was a good chance the cop wouldn't be able to prove anything. He picked up the safe cracker. 'Are you sure you didn't pick this up at the hospital' he said putting the ends in his ears.

'Don't get smart. You know damn well what it is. And the rest of it too'.

Zak picked up the rest of the tools and looked at them one by one as if he'd never seen them before. He couldn't understand why Gibbons was being so stupid, letting him examine all the items. He had a good excuse if they found his fingerprints on them now.

'Looks like some kind of tool kit' said Zak innocently. 'And you say that I was carrying these? It doesn't make any sense. I wasn't fixing my car or anything'. He could tell he was winning. Gibbons was looking despondent. He had hoped to get a confession out of Zak but things weren't going to plan.

'OK, so what were you doing with the mask then? I suppose you were going to a Halloween party'.

'What mask?'. Zak was getting confused. Why had Gibbons produced the tools but not the mask. Perhaps he had lost it. He was certainly dense enough.

'The one that you had in your pocket' said Gibbons. He had sent the mask to the station to see if it could be matched to any recent crimes. He liked to be one step ahead. He had a man working on it as they spoke, going through old files to see if anything came up.

'I'm sorry, but I don't know what you are talking about' said Zak.

'You were carrying a mask' said Gibbons impatiently. 'It was a latex mask. Generally used as a disguise'.

'Was it with the tools? Seems like a strange thing for someone to give me'. He smiled sweetly at the policeman who was getting annoyed.

'Do you honestly expect me to believe that someone would mug you and shower you with all of this', he waved his hand frantically at the tools as he spoke, 'and then vanish without taking your wallet?'

'What are you implying?' asked Zak innocently. 'What do you think I was doing?'

'Never mind'. Gibbons got up and paced around the room, thinking. If he could only find something to prove that Zak was up to no good. He glanced at the pile of clothes and saw that his jeans had gone missing. He knew they were there before as he had helped the nurse undress Zak and they had struggled with the jeans due to the rain soaking into them. They had left them until last, so they should have been on top of the pile. There was only one place they could be.

'In a hurry to leave, are you?' he asked.

'I've got nothing planned' replied Zak 'I expect I'll be kicked out before too long. You know, lack of hospital beds, lack of nurses. I'll probably stay for a few hours. Couple of aspirins to sort out my headache and I'll be fine'. He shuffled in the bed to get more comfortable. He wished he hadn't put the jeans on now.

'I was just wondering why you had started to get dressed. Seems a bit odd to put on a pair of wet jeans and jump back into bed if you are not going anywhere'. The policeman paced back and forth as he spoke. He liked to think it gave him an air of authority. He stopped and looked Zak straight in the eyes. 'Not planning a quick getaway, were we?'.

Zak opened his mouth to reply but was saved by a beeping sound. Gibbons turned off his pager and looked around for a phone.

'I'm not finished with you McDonald. Make sure you don't decide to do a runner'.

With that he strolled out of the ward calling to anyone who might be listening. 'Can you tell me where I can find a phone?'

Zak stared after him bemused. He'd met some strange people in his time but had never met anyone quite like Gibbons. He remembered an old friend once telling him that the police force was made up entirely of the tall people that left college and couldn't get a job. They only joined up for a laugh. This particular friend was a couple of inches on the short side so joined the army instead.

With a few minutes to himself, Zak started piecing together the events leading up to his chat with the deranged policeman. He supposed the money had been stolen when he was attacked. He would have been in deep trouble if the policeman had found him with a large wad of cash on him. Even Gibbons could put two and two together. It wouldn't have been a first offence either. He had been caught before trying to break into the cinema opposite the police station. He was only eighteen and, at the time it had seemed like a good dare. All he had to do was break in, steal one of the chairs from row W, and get out again. No problem. Except that there wasn't a row W. The back row was T. If he had given up there and then he wouldn't have been caught. But he decided to be clever. An upside-down chair from row M would probably do! The security guard caught him leaving an emergency exit with a chair clearly labelled 91W on his back. He had been dragged to the nearby police station and spent most of the night sitting on the chair he'd just pinched.

That time he had been let off with a warning. It was the only time he had been caught and he vowed never to do something so stupid again. Being mugged on the way home from a robbery wasn't classed as stupid in his book. Not very clever, admittedly, but not stupid.

He groaned as Gibbons walked back in. The policeman had a definite spring in his step and a wide grin had spread across his face.

'Mr McDonald' he said cheerfully. 'I'm arresting you under suspicion of the murder of Mr Don Connor. Anything you say may be taken down in evidence….'.

Zak didn't hear the rest. His mouth dropped open in amazement and his head started to swim.

Chapter 5 – "Get him out of there…"

Zak sat in his tiny cell in a daze. His head was still pounding. The aspirin he had taken hadn't done a lot of good, and he couldn't quite grasp the predicament he was in. He had been brought to the police station straight from the hospital and was promptly fingerprinted, photographed and left in the cell. He had tried to explain on several occasions the he'd not murdered anyone, that he wasn't even capable of murder, and that PC Gibbons was a couple of spanners short of a toolkit and must have made a mistake. No one had paid him the slightest bit of attention. He was just beginning to think that this was an elaborate ploy to get him to confess to the robbery when he was dragged back upstairs to the interview room.

He settled into the hard-wooden chair in the interview room and Gibbons walked in with another policeman. The second policeman ducked as he came through the door. He was huge. He could have played basketball for the NBA thought Zak. He wouldn't even need to jump!

'Good morning sir. My name is officer Peterson, you've already met officer Gibbons. We'd like to ask you a few questions regarding the murder of a Mr Don Connor'. Peterson had a deep menacing voice. He could drag a confession out of anyone thought Zak.

'OK. I'll answer any questions you want to ask me' said Zak. No point in aggravating the situation. He didn't want to get on the wrong side of Peterson.

'Where were you last night from midnight onwards?'. Peterson stared directly at him as he spoke, watching his every move.

'I left my house at about half past twelve' began Zak. He had had plenty of time to come up with a story that was as close to the truth as possible. He didn't want to confess to the robbery unless he had to. He would only confess if it looked like the murder was going to be pinned on him and he could use it as an alibi. 'I was having trouble sleeping so I went for a walk. I ended up in the town centre and just wandered around for a while'.

'Where did you go exactly? Just wandered round doesn't help us very much'.

'I remember walking past the "Sheep's Head" and heading down the high street towards the centre of town. I don't remember much after that. I woke up in hospital several hours later'.

'Did you see anyone in town?'

'No'.

'Did you see who hit you?'

'No. I heard a shout just before I was hit. I didn't get a chance to turn around. I was hit from behind'.

'Why were you carrying the tools?'

'I told officer Gibbons earlier, I've never seen them before'.

'And the mask?'

'Same thing. I haven't even seen this mask yet'. Zak was careful to point this out in case Gibbons jumped on him.

'These items were found in various pockets of the jacket you are wearing. I presume the clothes you are wearing are your own?'. Peterson was very sure of himself. He jotted down the odd note but most of the time he watched Zak like a hawk, looking for any slight twitch or hesitation.

'The clothes are mine'. Zak couldn't expect them to believe that he had been stripped of all his clothes and redressed in someone else's. He didn't want to push his luck too far.

'Have you ever been to a shop called View-it Videos?'

'The video rental shop? Yes. I have hired the odd video out from there'. Zak was thinking back to the video camera. What sort of picture could it produce in the dark shop? He had never worried about cameras before as the mask covered any distinct features. It had never occurred to him that he could be mugged and found by a policeman while he was still wearing the same clothes. He began to get a little anxious.

'Did you know Mr Connor, the manager?'

'I knew the guy in the shop was the manager. I didn't know his name. I never really spoke to him. Only when I hired a video out'.

'When was the last time you visited the shop?' Peterson leaned forward and studied Zak's face closer. Zak leaned back slightly without even realising he had done it. He began to sweat.

'Must have been a couple of weeks back, at least' he said.

Peterson stood up without taking his eyes off Zak and paced around the table. Zak had to crane his neck to look at the policeman's face. After a couple of seconds, he gave up and looked at Gibbons instead. Peterson crouched down beside Zak.

'Are you sure you didn't visit Mr Connor last night?' he said. 'Perhaps you are not thinking hard enough. Maybe the bump on your head has affected your thought process'.

'I didn't see Mr Connor last night' said Zak. 'I went for a walk. I got mugged. I spent all morning in hospital, and I came here'.

'Roll the video', said Peterson with a sigh, getting up.

Gibbons slid back part of the wall which was concealing a small television and video player. He pressed a couple of buttons and the TV sprung to life. A cold shiver passed through Zak as he saw a picture of the video shop clearly on the screen. In the bottom left hand corner was a digital clock showing 01:00.

The only thing that changed for a couple of minutes was the clock. Zak waited patiently, his mind racing. Then he saw it and his heart sank. In clear view, he saw himself walk into the shop and give a cheeky wave to the camera. Gibbons paused the video.

'Take a good look' said Peterson. 'Perhaps you might recognise the mask now. It goes quite nicely with that jacket and jeans you are wearing'.

'OK' sad Zak resignedly. 'I broke into the video store and pinched a few quid from the safe. Mr Connor wasn't there. It was one o'clock in the morning. Why would he be there at that hour?'

'He was working late. What did you kill him? Did he see you? Perhaps he recognised you?'

'He wasn't there. How could I kill him if he wasn't there?'. Zak pointed at the video. 'Have you watched the tape? Did you see me kill him? No. I know you didn't, because I didn't do it'.

'Mr McDonald, look at the time on the clock. You broke in at 01:02. You walk out the back to the storeroom'. Peterson walked to the video and pressed the play button. Zak watched himself walk into the storeroom. 'Right, you came out of the storeroom at 01:08. Six minutes. Watch the video'.

He put the video onto fast search, and they all watched the clock on the screen move up. At 01:08, he pressed play again. A few seconds later, Zak saw himself walk out of the storeroom and into the shop. Peterson stopped the video.

'Do you agree you were in the storeroom between 01:02 and 01:08?' he asked.

'Yes' said Zak. 'I was breaking into the safe. It took me several minutes. I grabbed some money and came out again. What makes you think that Connor was still there, and I killed him?'

Peterson took a plastic bag out of his pocket and emptied the contents onto the table in front of Zak.

'It's a watch' said Zak. 'Looks like it's seen better days'.

'This watch belonged to Mr Connor. It was bought for him by his wife. She has identified it'. Peterson paused. 'She told us that he was working on the computer in the store last night and was expecting to be very late. His body was found early this morning in the back of the storeroom. The same storeroom that you have just admitted you were in between the hours of 01:02 and 01:08. He was strangled. What do you notice about the watch?'.

'It's broken' said Zak. He still couldn't see how he was linked to this murder. 'I presume it got broke when he was attacked'.

'Exactly. Can you read the time?'

Zak squinted at the watch through the zigzags of broken glass and looked in disbelief. The watch read 01:03.

****

'You said it was urgent. Did you have any problems?'

'Not with Connor. I was in and out in minutes. Nobody saw me'.

'So why are you so worried? If nobody saw you, we haven't got any problems'.

'The shop was burgled just after I left'. The guy was caught and….well – to cut a long story short, he's about to get life for murder'.

'So, what's the problem? Case closed. They won't be looking for anyone now'.

'The guy was Zak McDonald'.

There was a long pause 'Get him out of there. Preferably unconscious. I'll think of something'. He hung up.

****

'Is that it? You drag a sick man down from the hospital on suspicion of murder and all you've got is a broken watch for evidence?'. Zak had stood up and was shouting furiously at the two policemen. He only came up to Peterson's chest which didn't make him as intimidating as he would have liked.

'Sid down McDonald' said Peterson impatiently. He waited until Zak was sitting again and leaned over him, placing his hands on either side of the chair looking down at him menacingly. 'You agreed that you were in the shop between 01:02 and 01:08' he said.

Zak nodded.

'Connor was attacked at 01:03. His broken watch tells us that. Nobody else was around. You told us yourself that you didn't see anyone. We've also got results from the post-mortem stating that he was killed between 12:30 and 01:30 this morning. And ', he stabbed Zak in the chest with his finger to make a point '...we have a video placing you at the scene of the crime within minutes of Connor being murdered. It seems to me that we have quite a lot of evidence to link you to this. Why don't you make life easy for us all and tell us what really happened? You'll get a lighter sentence if you cooperate and plead guilty'.

Zak was getting worried. His outburst hadn't phased Peterson at all and he had to admit that they had a pretty strong case against him.

'Surely it's all circumstantial though' he said, a little desperately. 'You haven't got any concrete proof that I killed him. I admit I broke into the shop, and I agree that it seems very likely that Connor was killed about the same time, but I didn't do it. Where's the motive? Why would I do such a thing? There must be something you've missed somewhere'.

'The video tape and watch are all the evidence we need' said Gibbons from the corner of the room. He hadn't said anything since they had come in and his voice startled Zak. 'Looks like you'll be going down for a very long time'.

Zak was taken back down to his cell, protesting his innocence all the way. After the door slammed shut behind him, he fell to the bed and cried for the first time in many years. He didn't see the man in the corner of the room step towards him and hit him on the back of the head with a heavy object. For the second time that day, he crumpled to the floor.

Chapter 6 – "What about the girl?"

Zak was dreaming again – A happy dream this time. He was at his wedding watching his bride walk slowly down the aisle towards him. She looked more beautiful than ever before, the long white dress flowing behind her making it appear as if she was floating on a cloud. Cameras were clicking and flashing, catching the moment – The happy faces, the tearful mothers and the little bridesmaids trying their hardest to walk in sync with one another.

She reached the front and turned to face Zak. He could smell her sweet perfume Coco Chanel – her favourite, and her long blonde hair sparkled as if it were alive. She lifted her veil slowly over her head and Zak gasped in horror. Her face was burnt to a crisp, the lips blistering and peeling away from the mouth, the eyes just round sockets staring vacantly at him. A vile liquid was dripping down from where her nose once was, and the smell of perfume was replaced with the revolting stench of burning flesh.

The dream started to fade, just as she stretched up towards him and gave him a kiss full on the mouth, her icy tongue just catching the tip of his and sending a shiver through his entire body. There was a spell of fuzziness as the image diminished and a new one replaced it. He was in a graveyard.....

….Zak shivered as he watched her body being slowly lowered into the ground. The weather had suddenly turned very cold and the nearby trees were swaying violently in the fierce wind. His mind raced back to the accident. The tyre exploding. The car hurtling across the road. The tree coming at an unimaginable speed towards the passenger door. He had fought the skid all the way, but it seemed that nothing was going to stop the collision. He had gone over it in his mind time and time again. Did he do something wrong? Could he have prevented it somehow? Was he going too fast? Had that second drink slowed his reflexes? The truth of the matter was that it was just a freak accident. A one in a million chance. He knew it, but couldn't let it lie, couldn't convince himself that he wasn't responsible for her death somehow. He had tortured himself every minute of the three weeks he lay in the hospital bed recovering. His shattered knee had recovered remarkably well. His broken heart would take a lot longer. The coffin dropped deeper and deeper and Zak turned away. He couldn't bare it anymore. The only woman he'd ever loved – taken from him, far too young.

He had visited her grave every day for a month, spent long hours just staring at the stone slab, remembering the days they had spent together. It had only been a few years, but it was in those few years that he had done everything he'd ever wanted to do. As he began to drift out of the dream, the words on the gravestone burned across his mind:-

Here lies Mary Ann McDonald
Born 01-06-1964
Died 31-05-1990
Loving wife to Zak

She had been killed the day before her twenty-sixth birthday.

Zak woke to find himself in pitch darkness, lying on something soft – probably a bed by the feel of it. It took him a while to realise that the reason it was so dark might be something to do with the blindfold he was wearing. He sat up, and the all too familiar pain shot back through his head, worse than it had been earlier. He tugged the blindfold off, only to find he was still in darkness. He felt for the edge of the bed and swung his legs over the side.

They didn't touch the floor.

It was a peculiar sensation, sitting in the dark, his legs dangling over the edge of….what? Was it a bed? Possibly - And not knowing how far down the floor was. He tried leaning over and stretching down as far as possible – but all he could feel was empty space. Probably a bunk bed, he thought. Only a few feet the ground. I could swing on to the lower bunk.

But what if it wasn't? What if he jumped down expecting to land on the bed below and there wasn't one there? He didn't relish the thought of throwing himself off without knowing for sure what was underneath. No way. This is crazy, he thought. How the hell did I get here? This can't be my cell. He felt around to see if he could gather any more information about his position and found a headboard at one end of the bed. So – It was a bed. Stop fooling around and jump down. There must be a light switch somewhere.

He prepared to leap down but couldn't bring himself to do it. Instead he got a firm grip on the side of the bed and dangled over the edge, his feet stretching down towards the ground.

He didn't find it.

He kicked out in front of him, expecting to come into contact with the lower bunk, but again there was nothing there. From a spectator's point of view, the situation would have been quite amusing, but Zak couldn't see the funny side. He hoisted himself back onto the bed and sat there taking deep breaths, his heart gradually slowing to a normal rhythm.

So, I can't go down, he thought. What about up?

He stretched upwards from his sitting position, but again all he found was air. He carefully stood up, and cracked his already painful head on the ceiling, causing him to collapse to the bed again. He nearly blacked out with the excruciating pain that followed. He had taken more blows to the head in this one day than he had for his entire life. It wasn't something he recommended.

After a few agonising minutes, he slowly reached up again and found the ceiling with his hands. He ran his fingers over the smooth surface looking for something, anything that might shed some light on the situation. He hit something solid and round, sticking vertically out of the ceiling and his fingers felt around it, following a path down to the bed. Upon further investigation, he found three more – one on each corner, keeping the bed securely fastened to the ceiling.

What the hell is this? he thought. I'm sitting on a bed that's bolted to the ceiling, and I can't see my own hands, let alone the floor. I should be in a nice cosy prison cell sleeping off this bloody headache, not stuck up here. He dropped back on to the bed and punched it in frustration, like a child throwing a tantrum. His hand hit something soft and he picked it up, recognising it as a pillow. He groped around but found nothing else. A sheet might have been more useful, he thought. Might be able to tie it to the post and climb down. How far down? He still had no idea.

He leaned over the edge of the bed again and dropped the pillow, listening for the impact with the floor. It came sooner than he expected. Still too far to jump, but maybe only fifteen to twenty feet – hard to be sure, but he could make it if he had a soft landing. He grabbed at the mattress and was pleased to find that it wasn't attached to the bed. He shuffled about and with some difficulty managed to lift it out from under him. He prepared to throw it over the side, when a thought struck him. What if it drifts slightly when it falls? There was a good chance he would miss it completely when he jumped. Probably better to wrap it around himself instead – at least he would have some protection.

The mattress was quite supple, and he managed to bend it around himself fairly well. He sat on the edge of the bed again, had a few false starts where he contemplated once again how foolish he must look, but finally threw himself to the unknown.

****

'McDonald was no problem. The cops think he escaped somehow and have set up a major search party'. He chuckled. 'I don't think they'll find him tonight though'.

'OK. What about the girl?'

'That could be tricky. She hasn't got a good reason to go missing. People will notice. We're trying to catch her when she's on her own. Save any complications'.

'We may not have a choice. Do what you have to. I'll do it myself if you run into problems. Let me know when you've got her'.

When the man had left the room, Ron Miller flicked a switch on the panel in front of him and a small monitor burst into life, producing a picture that was completely black. He hit another switch and a glow appeared on the screen as the infrared camera kicked in. The picture showed Zak wrapped in a mattress, high up, contemplating his jump. He watched with interest, a smile forming on his lips as Zak leapt.

****

The landing could have been better. He hit the ground hard, the mattress taking some of the sting out, but the impact was still enough to make him cry out loud. He lay dazed on the floor, his shoulder now throbbing in time with his head. It was good to be on solid ground again, even though he couldn't see it.

He waited for the worst of the pain to subside before sliding himself backwards along the floor. If he was going to explore the room he was in, it would be best to start at the wall and hunt for a light switch. He had only travelled about four feet when his hand touched the cold wall behind him. He straightened up and slowly began to walk around the room, his hands never leaving the wall he was on. After about two minutes of walking, he hadn't reached the corner of the room. This must be one hell of a large room, he thought. Even at the slow pace he was going, he estimated he had travelled at least fifty feet. He carried on for another two minutes, but still hadn't found anything. OK, so it must be a corridor. Why would there be a bed high up in the air at the end of a corridor? It didn't make sense. He reached out in front of him and walked slowly forwards, heading for the other side of the corridor, but after a few steps he tripped over the mattress.

He groaned as the penny dropped. He'd been walking around in circles. A few steps in each direction confirmed this as he reached a wall on every side. So where was the door? Where was the light switch? He'd been round the room several times and all he'd felt was the cold, slightly damp wall.

'Having fun Mr McDonald'. The deep voice made Zak jumped as it echoed around the small room. He spun around frantically looking for its owner.

'Peterson? Is that you? Where the hell have you put me? I could have killed myself falling from that bed'. Zak didn't think it was Peterson, but he wanted to keep the man talking to try and work out where he was.

'Yes - The bed. Interesting way of getting down. I rather enjoyed that. Did you hurt yourself?'

The voice didn't give any indication of concern. It was merely mocking him.

'I'll live' muttered Zak. 'I don't suppose you want to turn a light on for me. Make my life a little bit easier'.

The man laughed, and the room was suddenly illuminated with a brilliant glow. Zak shielded his eyes. It was almost blinding after being in the darkness for so long, and his head gave him another twinge reminding him that it was by no means recovered. When he had got accustomed to the light, he scanned the room.

There wasn't much to see. As he had deduced, he was in a perfectly round room about ten foot across. The walls were a dazzling white colour and they stretched up about twenty-five foot. On the wall, opposite where he stood was the bed, high up, suspended from the ceiling. It was quite a drop. He was sure he wouldn't have jumped if he'd seen how high up he really was. Opposite the bed was a small wall mounted camera watching his every move. The floor was also white and bare, except for the pillow and the mattress which were covering the centre of the room.

He looked around again. Where was the way in? He must have got in here somehow. There were no doors or windows anywhere. He looked up at the bed again. How did they get him up there?

'It's fascinating isn't it? You could look for ages and never find the door. Perhaps I should give you a clue'. Ron paused, watching Zak look despairingly around to see where the voice was coming from. 'Or perhaps not. No, I think I'll let you work it out on your own. You did get off that bed without any clues, and it was dark then. You have light now. It should be a doddle for a man of your means'.

'What am I doing here? How did I get here?'. Zak had a million questions to ask and the man wasn't giving him any answers.

'We'll talk later. You must be hungry. I'll leave a meal out for you. You'll find it outside the door'.

There was a click and the room fell silent.

Chapter 7 – "Conspicuous"

Julie Morris looked at her watch again and cursed British Rail – as she always did when her train was late. This had been happening more and more often just lately and she wondered if it was worth the hassle of travelling to London every day to work. Sure, the extra money came in handy – but it wasn't like her old job which she could walk to in five minutes and never have to suffer the perils of public transport.

An announcement was coming over the tannoy, but she couldn't decipher it. Somebody apologising about something for the delay of some train or other. She hoped it wasn't hers. If she was late to work again, she could kiss her promotion prospects goodbye for good. She had hoped to get it when the last senior secretary had left, but the position had been filled by Linda Rivers. Linda was only average in her opinion, and Julie had resented the fact that she been overlooked, and the job had gone to Linda. It was only because she had walked around the office in low-cut dresses, sucking up to all the people that mattered. Making their coffee and fluttering her eyelashes whenever she thought it would get her somewhere. It had worked. Julie had not even been considered. She had doubled her efforts since then, and it was looking like it would pay off at last. A decision wasn't being made until the end of the week, but she was fairly confident that she had it in the bag.

That's if she could get to work on time.

Her train slowly trundled into the station five minutes later. It was running over ten minutes late by the time it pulled away again. It didn't even appear to be hurrying, thought Julie. The train should be hurtling towards London around about now. It certainly would be if she had anything to do with it.

She took a magazine out of her bag, sighed and crossed her legs as she read her horoscope. Nothing interesting – not that she believed in it anyway. It informed her that she was to be careful of her money and to watch out for a stranger wearing blue. Who wrote this rubbish anyway? Probably someone sitting in a cosy little office and getting paid a damn site more than she did. She turned the page, found a pen in her jacket pocket and settled down to do the crossword.

The train was running fifteen minutes late by the time it pulled up at Waterloo. Julie leapt off before it had even stopped and ran through the station holding up her season ticket to anyone who happened to pass. She nearly lost a shoe as she darted through the turnstile leading to the Central line of the underground. As she arrived on the platform, the tube was pulling out of site into the dark tunnel.

'Shit', she said under her breath, a look of disgust spreading across her face. She trudged to a seat and sat down to wait for the next one, glancing at her watch as she did so - 8:52. She'd be lucky to get to work by ten past at the earliest.

A man stepped up to the bench, wiped the seat and sat down beside her.

'It's typical isn't it?' he said. 'You get up at the crack of dawn to go to a job over fifty miles away, and the trains let you down. You don't do anything wrong yourself, but you still get there late – and you have to take the shit for it'.

Julie nodded a polite yes, but didn't want to be drawn into a conversation with him. He was wearing blue – good enough reason not to talk to him in her opinion. The man was more persistent though.

'Are you running late too? I saw you looking at your watch. Bloody trains are all the same. Still, I suppose that's the price you pay for working in the city'.

Julie nodded again and gave him a slight smile. She didn't need this. She reached down and retrieved the magazine from her bag and turned her attention back to the crossword. The man didn't speak for about 30 seconds. Then….

'Conspicuous'.

'Sorry?' she said.

'Four down. "Attracting attention". It's conspicuous. See?'. He pointed to the place where it fit in the crossword and started spelling it out for her.

'C....O...N. "

'Oh Yes, thanks". She couldn't believe the guy. How did she end up sitting next to this cretin? She looked around for the train but there was no sign of it.

'Do you need a pen? I've got one here somewhere'. He opened his briefcase and started rummaging through various documents and papers before she could speak. 'I know it's in here somewhere. Just give me a minute. You wouldn't believe the rubbish I carry in here. I always do though. Never know when you might need something'.

He picked up a manky looking toothbrush and looked at it with delight.

'That's where it went' he exclaimed. Do you know – I've been looking for that for days. Have you ever tried brushing your teeth when you haven't got a brush? It's a nightmare – I can tell you'.

He dropped the toothbrush back in and continued to search for the pen.

'Don't worry about it' said Julie. 'I have one somewhere. I'll fill it in later at work'. This was getting embarrassing. People had begun to look and point, sniggering at the eccentric man in the blue anorak. She didn't want them to think that she was with him.

'Here it is', he said triumphantly, producing a pen from his mass of papers and passing it to her. She took it quickly and started writing the word in her magazine. She reached the "P" when the pen ran out.

'Would you believe it?' he said in amazement. 'I've only had it about a week. I bet it was the one that everyone tries out in the shop. I've a good mind to take it back and get a replacement. I might even ask for my money back. It could be a bad batch. You never know'.

He grabbed the pen off her and shook it vigorously up and down.

'Try it now. That might do the trick'.

She reached the second "O" when it ran out again. She could have happily stuck the pen up the man's nose – or even somewhere else, she thought to herself. Why does this sort of stuff always happen to me? Of all the people on the platform, why did it have to be me?

She heaved a sigh of relief as she saw the train coming.

'Not to worry. I'll do it later' she said, putting the magazine back into her bag and handing the pen back to him.

As he took it, the briefcase slipped off his lap and the contents fell out. Several papers fluttered off down the platform with the rush of the train, and he let out a cry of despair and leapt up after them. Julie pretended not to notice, and hurriedly boarded the train. As it pulled into the tunnel, she saw him running down the platform chasing after a document and planting a foot on it just before it fell onto the tracks. She tried hard not to laugh but couldn't stop herself and turned away so he wouldn't see. You're a bad person Julie Morris, she thought. He was only being helpful.

It had cheered her up though. Perhaps the day wasn't going to be so bad after all.

****

She was lucky. Her boss was running late too, and she beat him into the office by two and a half minutes. She had covered the quarter mile walk to the office in just over 2 minutes and her heart was still racing when he strolled in.

'Morning Julie' he called to her as he passed. 'Any calls?'

'Morning Bob. Not yet. It's been quiet since I arrived'. She was still a bit breathless, but he didn't seem to notice.

'Ah, good. Just what I wanted. A peaceful day. Will help me wind down for the holiday'. His spirits lifted at the thought. He was taking his wife on a surprise trip to Japan for their twenty-fifth wedding anniversary. It was the one place they had always talked about going to, but never quite made it. There was always some excuse for going somewhere else.

'Do you have to remind me?' groaned Julie. 'I'll be slaving away at work while you're living it up on the other side of the world'.

'Isn't it a shame. I'll send you a postcard if you're lucky'.

He sauntered off into his office with a big grin on his face.

Julie smiled. She was pleased to see him in a good mood. He was a workaholic who stayed later than her every night and worked most Saturdays too. He deserved the holiday and she was glad he was getting away for a couple of weeks, even if she had to put up with his constant reminders and sarcastic remarks.

She switched on her computer and settled down to finish a letter she had started the day before. The letter was printing when Bob appeared with a tape for her to type up.

'No peace for the wicked', she grumbled handing him the letter. 'I suppose this is extremely urgent and it's imperative that I type it up before I do anything else'.

It was always the case whoever gave her work to do. Whether it was typing, arranging meetings or even making coffee, it seemed it was always the number one priority.

Bob laughed. 'Of course it is. Don't worry. It's not very long. I'm sure that for someone as efficient and hard working as you, it will be done by ten o'clock'.

'Hmm' she said getting out the small tape player. 'That means it will take me until lunchtime at least'

'Oh. Nearly forgot' said Bob handing her a second tape. 'The rest of it is on this one'. He scarpered quick.

'Ten o'clock? You must be joking. I'll be here till....'. He didn't hear the rest.

She was just queueing up the tape when Tom Roberts dropped a memo on her desk needing some alterations.

'Any chance you can slip this one in urgently?' he asked.

Julie gave him a look that could kill, and he grabbed it back.

'Oh. Erm – Never mind, I'll see if Linda can do it' he said retreating quickly.

She smiled. 'Good choice Tom. You're learning quicker every day'.

He grinned and wandered down the office in search of Linda. Julie pressed play on the tape player and nearly fell off her chair when she heard Bob singing a rather bad rendition of Cliff Richard.

'We're all going on a summer holiday. No more working for a week or two'.

She was still laughing when the dictation started, and she had to wind back and start again.

After many other interruptions, the letter took the best part of the day to complete. As she was tidying her desk ready to go home, Bob popped his head around his office door.

'Have you got a minute?' he said.

She quickly stuck the rest of her things away and went into his office.

'I'm not in for the rest of the week. Got some packing to do. Did I tell you I was going away?'

'No' she said feigning surprise. 'Where on Earth could you be going?'

He laughed. 'Seeing as I won't be here, I wanted to give you some good news...but following the sarcasm, I might just wait till I'm back'. He had a wicked glint in his eye.

'You wouldn't dare' she said. 'Now that I'm here, you have to tell me. I won't let you out the door if you don't. She tried to put on a serious expression, but it didn't quite come off.

Bob smiled and handed her an envelope. She tore it open and read the letter inside. She had got the promotion. From next Monday she would be a senior secretary.

'Congratulations' said Bob. 'I wanted to tell you early as I won't be here to wish you good luck'.

'Thanks'. She was grinning from ear to ear. 'I'm going to miss working for you though. I'll have nobody to antagonize'.

'Oh, I'm sure you'll find someone' he replied.

'Well, if I don't, I'll be down here on my coffee break. You'd better watch your back'.

'At least I'll be safe for two weeks. Did I tell you...'

'Yes'. She cut him off promptly. 'Aren't you going to Japan for a fortnight? I think I heard you mention it'.

'Perhaps I did once or twice'. He laughed. 'Anyway, keep up the good work. You deserved the promotion. Long overdue in my opinion. I think you'll be fine working for John'.

'Thanks. I hope you have a wonderful holiday. Have you told Mel yet?' Mel was Bob's wife.

'No. I'll have to tell her tonight though. I'm taking her out for a meal. She doesn't even know that I've got the rest of the week off'.

'It's alright for some'. She got up. 'I suppose I'd better get a move on. I expect the train will be late again though. See you in a couple of weeks. Have fun'.

'Yes. If I decide to come back'.

She walked out of his office laughing. Now, if only he was about twenty years younger and single. She could do a lot worse. She put her coat on and headed for the station.

****

The rest of the week was fairly uneventful. The office was quiet with Bob away and the trains were surprisingly on time for a change. She spotted blue anorak guy in the distance one day at the tube station but managed to duck behind a busker playing a dreary version of "American Pie" on a five stringed guitar. She got home Friday night, and phoned her best friend Jenny.

'Fancy going out for a drink? My treat' she said.

'You're paying? Are you ill? What's the occasion?'. Jenny couldn't believe it. Julie never offered to pay.

'I'll tell you later. Can you make it round here for eight?'

'I can't' said Jenny sadly. 'I promised my mum I'd take her to my grans, and I've already cancelled once. I can't let her down again. Tomorrow?'

'OK. I'll run a bath and have a lazy evening. I'm sure the celebrations can wait one evening'.

'Are you going to tell me what this is all about?'

'No. You can wait until tomorrow. Where do you want to go?'

'Well, since you're paying, I'd better let you decide' said Jenny.

'OK. We'll start at "The Magpie". If you get around here for about eight o'clock I should be ready'.

'That means about eight forty-five knowing you'. Jenny knew what Julie was like.

'No. I'll be ready for eight. Promise. You can trust me'.

'Last time you said that you were running over an hour late' said Jenny. 'You blamed it on the train. You always use that as an excuse, but you can't this time'.

'I'll be ready. Don't worry. See you tomorrow night'.

'Still not gonna tell me?'

'Tomorrow. Bye'.

Julie hung up. A quiet night in wouldn't hurt. She put some music on and went to run herself a hot bath.

Chapter 8 – "Up, Down Flush"

Zak scanned the room again looking for any form of escape route. He had eliminated the idea that the door was at ground level and was now looking higher. With the walls being such a brilliant white colour, he figured that any entrance would show up quite clearly. Even if the room had a white sliding door, the edges would be visible. After a good ten minutes peering up and down, he began to think that the walls had been built around him.

He sank onto the mattress and frowned in despair. He was missing something obvious and couldn't work out what it was. He lay there staring up at the ceiling, occasionally glancing at the camera.

Another few minutes passed, and it suddenly occurred to him that he was probably being hunted down by every policeman in the country. He didn't believe for a second that his current situation had anything to do with the police. They wouldn't leave him stranded like this. Nothing but a bed with a mattress and a pillow. No door, no toilet. Not even a window to look out of. His mind jumped back a couple of seconds.

Wait - no toilet!

It was something that he hadn't considered, but as time slipped by, he realised that it could become a very major problem. Surely, they would let him out for that. Wouldn't they? The thought was enough to get him moving and he jumped up and started to scan the room again.

After what seemed like the tenth time around the room, he began to get annoyed. He had even gone around the walls, tapping them to see if any part was hollow, but nothing was out of the ordinary. Out of desperation, he started examining the pillow to see if there was anything inside it.

There wasn't.

He tossed it aside and was about to grab the mattress when he realised that since the light had come on, it had been in the same place, covering the centre of the floor.

He hadn't checked the floor.

He had been around the room so many times he had lost count – and not once had it occurred to him that there might be something on the floor. He held his breath in anticipation and dragged the mattress to the side of the room.

There was a trapdoor.

It was painted white like the rest of the room but had a little silver ring in the middle so it could be opened inwards. He could have kicked himself. He must have walked over it several times. He was even laying over it at one point! He stared at it in amazement. What a crazy place to put the only entrance to the room, he thought. Who in their right mind would put a door in the middle of the floor?

He grabbed the ring and pulled. It didn't budge. Is it locked? Have I really searched this room for half an hour only to finally find a door that I can't open? He put both hands on the ring and tugged harder. The trapdoor moved up and then down a fraction of an inch, but it was plain to see that something was securing it down. As he tugged, he noticed that the ring turned slightly. He stopped pulling and began turning the ring instead. After a couple of rotations, he heard a click. He tugged the ring and the trapdoor flew open.

The first thing he noticed was a screwdriver attached to the roof of the trapdoor. Odd!

The next thing he noticed was that it wasn't the way out. It was just an empty space with a hole in it, about ten inches in diameter. By the side of the hole were three buttons. One was marked "Up", one was marked "Down". The third was marked "Flush".

He'd found the toilet.

****

Ron was still watching Zak, grinning when he tapped the walls and applauding the small screen mockingly when he finally found the trap door. He had been worried that Zak wouldn't be able to cope with some of the plans that he had for him, but after watching him in action, his fears had begun to subside.

'It seems that our Mr. McDonald is far more resourceful then I first thought' he said. 'Have you got a meal prepared for him? He won't be in there much longer'.

'Food's ready. Do you think we'll be able to contain him? He's used to breaking in to places. I'm sure he could break out of the whole complex given half the chance'.

'That's that part I'm looking forward to. The fun doesn't start until he gets outside. I'm just playing with him until our Dear Miss Morris is brought in'. Ron robbed his hands together. 'If we can get the timing right, our assignment will be as good as completed. No harm in having a bit of fun in the meantime'.

He swivelled his chair back to the screen in front of him and turned his attention back to Zak.

****

Zak looked at the toilet in amazement. He'd seen it all now. A toilet under a trapdoor in a room with no door and a bed hanging from the ceiling. It all seemed like a silly dream. He would wake up in a minute and find himself recovering from a sore head in his tiny cell. He closed his eyes and counted to sixty. He was still there when he opened them again. OK – Not a dream.

He looked at the three buttons – Up, down and flush. He had a pretty good idea what the "Flush" button was for but couldn't understand what possible use the other two had. He pressed the "Up" button. Nothing happened, so he pressed the "Down" button instead. He heard a slight whirring noise from behind him, but it stopped when he let go of the button. He turned around.

The bed had dropped about a foot.

He pressed the "Down" button again and held it until the bed reached the floor. He pressed the "Up" button and watched the bed go up again. He laughed out loud in disbelief. What possible use was this? He could make the bed go up and down. Big deal! For my next trick, I'll levitate the pillow.

He pressed the button marked "Flush", and the toilet did exactly that. No surprises there. He brought the bed back down to the floor and sat on it. He didn't notice the entrance at the top of the wall until he lay back on the bed.

Zak sat bolt upright again. Where did that come from? It wasn't there last time he looked. It suddenly dawned on him that the entrance had been concealed by the bed. When the bed was at the top of the wall, the headboard covered the hole completely. All he had to do was take the bed back up and remove the headboard. It sounded too simple.

It wasn't.

He couldn't press the "Up" button and be on the bed at the same time. He sat and pondered the situation for a minute.

He got up, and then sat down again frowning. He was so close. He'd found the way out but couldn't reach it. He looked up at the hole in the wall and tried to estimate how far up it was. An idea came to him.

He jumped off the bed and returned to the trapdoor and raised the bed about ten foot up the wall. Then he leapt, making a grab for the edge but fell a couple of inches short. After a few attempts, he lowered the bed a bit and tried again. This time he reached it and hoisted himself up and stood on it, reaching his hand up the wall. He was still about six feet below the hole. He made a desperate jump for it but knew that he wasn't going to make it, nearly falling off in the process. OK – bad idea. He didn't want another knock on the head.

He jumped off the bed and brought it back down to the floor. There must be a way of wedging the button down, he thought. He didn't have much at hand that might be useful.

Then he remembered the screwdriver.

He picked it up and put the end of it on the "Up" button. Then he grabbed the pillow, placed it over the screwdriver, and gently lowered the trapdoor lid on top of the pillow.

Nothing happened. There wasn't quite enough weight on the button. He dragged the mattress over to the trapdoor and placed it on top of everything.

The bed began to rise.

He dashed to the bed and threw himself on it. As it rose, he congratulated himself for his ingenuity. He had had to use everything in the room to do it, but he was finally going to get out of this wretched place.

The bed reached the hole and carried on past. He nearly risked jumping through while the bed was moving but didn't fancy getting trapped or squashed. Decapitated even. It was moving fairly quickly, and the hole wasn't huge. The bed came to a stop covering the hole and he grabbed at the headboard.

It was stuck fast.

He couldn't believe it. He figured a good tug would have ripped it straight off, but it didn't seem to be the case. He pulled it one way, then the other. He lay on his back and gave it a few swift kicks. The headboard didn't want to know. He leaned over the edge and looked underneath, groaning at what he saw. The headboard was secured by six screws.

'What didn't I take it off first?', he moaned in exasperation. 'How could I be so stupid?'

He moaned even louder when he realised that he would have to jump again – and without the soft landing. At least he could see this time.

After another painful jump, it was fairly easy work. Lower the bed, retrieve the screwdriver, unscrew the headboard, and set up everything again. The bed rose once more, and he heaved a sigh of relief as the hole came closer. When it stopped, he hopped through and into another room.

****

He had walked into what appeared to be a kitchen. There was a meal set out as promised on a large wooden table with a hard, wooden chair next to it. He sat down to eat while he examined the rest of the room. Like the bedroom – if you could call it that, the whole place was a dazzling white, but it was broken up with splashes of colour here and there – almost as if a small child had got a bit slap happy with a paintbrush. There was a sink in the corner and a fridge next to it. The fridge had a magnet attached to it, holding a digital clock. The time was 10:17. He figured it was probably evening but couldn't be sure because, again the room was windowless. There was a microwave oven on top of a row of pine kitchen units with an empty microwave dish next to it. It looked like Zak's meal had only just been made.

The food wasn't very appetizing, but Zak ate it anyway. He hadn't eaten for over twenty-four hours and hadn't noticed how hungry he was until now. The meal consisted of a measly piece of meat – possibly pork, a few vegetables and a couple of roast potatoes that tasted like they were made out of cardboard and had the texture of recently set cement. He still cleaned his plate off though, and when he found the fridge full of similar meals, he cooked another one and ate that too.

Feeling a little better, he had a quick look through all the cupboards and drawers to see if he could find anything useful. Most of them were empty, but he did come across a bunch of keys and various types of cutlery. He took a knife and fork and put them in his pocket. Might be able to use them as a weapon, he mused. He grabbed the keys and pocketed them too.

He found a larder that he'd missed on his first inspection. It was stacked full of soup, baked beans, a few vegetables and some other canned food. At least I won't go hungry, he thought. There was also a mop and bucket, a length of rope, a large washing up bowl, some washing up liquid and some matches. He couldn't understand why they would equip him with all these items. He didn't know if he could use them in any way to escape but considered for a brief moment trying to set light to the mattress to see what effect it would have.

He refrained.

He was just turning away when something caught his eye. He picked it up and examined it. It appeared to be some sort of a gun. It looked like a gun in every way. Same shape, same features – except that it didn't appear to have a hole in the barrel. Zak lifted the gun, aimed it at the plate he had just eaten off and pulled the trigger.

Nothing happened.

Or that's what he first thought, but then noticed that a very thin beam of light was emerging from the end of the gun. A laser gun? He dismissed that idea straight away. This wasn't a laser. It was just a beam of light – like a glorified torch really. He found a light switch and turned the lights off and tried the gun again. This time he could see it clearly. A thin red beam emanating from the end of the gun and onto the wall at the end of the room. He shrugged and switched the lights on again. After seeing a bed that rose up and down and a toilet under a trapdoor, he wasn't overly surprised to see a gun shaped torch. He put it in his pocket with the knife, fork and keys. Maybe he would find a use for it later. Who knows?

It was then that he realised that this room actually had a door in it. No hidden holes, no concealed entrances. Just a normal everyday door. He tried it, and it opened – revealing a solid brick wall. He laughed. Hardly surprising really, he thought. He had got used to the idea that he was being kept prisoner, however strange the prison was.

'I hope you enjoyed your meal Mr McDonald'. The voice was back, and it made him jump again.

'It's hardly worth a compliment, but for prison food it was passable', he replied sarcastically. 'Are you going to keep me in suspense or are you going to tell me why I'm here?'

'In time. In time. You shouldn't see this place as a prison. We saved you from prison – remember? This place is more like, how shall I put it? A holiday camp'.

'A bloody holiday camp?' fumed Zak. 'Where the hell do you go for your holidays? Aren't you supposed to enjoy yourself at a holiday camp?' Zak had found the camera on the wall and was shouting directly at it, waving his arms up and down to help emphasise his anger.

'We'd *like* you to enjoy yourself. You won't come to any harm. We decided we needed you for an experiment. Everything will become apparent in time. You should relax and enjoy yourself in the meantime'.

'Enjoy myself? How am I supposed to enjoy myself when I'm trapped in a place like this? What gives you the right to drag me here and use me in your experiments anyway?'

'Let's just say that nobody else can give us the result we would like'. Anyway, I've told you far too much for one night. You should be feeling sleepy by now. You did eat all of your food didn't you?'

Zak's eyes had begun to get heavy and now he knew why. They had spiked his food.

'We couldn't have you running around tonight. We felt it necessary to help you get a good night's sleep. It would be wise to do so. You'll need all of your strength for tomorrow'. He paused. 'If you make your way back to your bed now, you'll be able to see where you're going. The lights are going off in exactly one minute. Good night. We'll talk in the morning'.

Zak stumbled back towards the hole. The sedative was really kicking in now and he didn't feel like sleeping on the floor. He'd be aching all over tomorrow if he did. He reached the bed, finding that there was no mattress or pillow.

'Give me another minute to get the mattress and pillow at least?' he said. There was no answer, but the bed started to drop.

Zak sorted his bed out and collapsed onto it just as he was plunged into darkness. His last thought before he passed out was that whoever was holding him was not alone. His captor had kept saying "We". Who were they? What did they want him for? He had no time to figure anything else out before he fell into unconsciousness.

Chapter 9 – "Fancy a toy boy"

Saturday was fairly boring. Julie did a bit of shopping, tidied the house and generally wasted the day. She was looking forward to a night on the town. She hadn't got really drunk for months, so tonight, she decided she was going to let her hair down a bit.

At seven o'clock, Julie went into her little bedroom to get ready. She rented a poky little one bedroomed flat that was barely big enough to swing a cat in. Still, with the promotion she might be able to get something a bit bigger. She smiled to herself. Her future was certainly looking brighter. All I need now is a bloke, she thought. Preferably rich, and handsome. They were the two most important things in her eyes.

She stripped off and had a quick shower in her tiny bathroom. If she tried to swing a cat in this particular room, it wouldn't have survived very long. All it contained was a bath with a shower over it and a sink that was overlapping the bath slightly due to lack of space. The toilet was in a separate room. As she was drying herself off, she examined herself in the mirror. Not bad for a twenty-eight-year-old, she thought. Could do with losing a bit of weight around the hips – but who can't? She sucked in her belly and held it, turning sideways to see the full effect. She had kept herself in good shape, playing tennis in the summer and she regularly visited the local sports centre to do a quick fifty laps of the pool. She returned to her bedroom and opened her cupboard, trying to find something suitable to wear.

At eight o'clock when Jenny arrived, she still hadn't made up her mind. She couldn't decide whether to dress up in her little black dress that she kept for special occasions or go more casual in a pair of jeans and sparkly top.

'I knew you wouldn't be ready. What did I tell you? You never are' moaned Jenny, sticking her hands on her hips and impersonating Julie's mother.

'I'm as good as ready. Here - Which shall I wear?'. Julie held up the two outfits against her in turn, posing like a model.

'I like the black one. If I'd known you were dressing up, then I wouldn't have worn these'. She indicated the denims she was wearing. 'Wear the jeans. You can't wear that in the pub. You'll have every bloke in there throwing himself at you. I won't stand a chance of pulling'.

'That's what I thought', said Julie, her eyes gleaming. 'It's a bit desperate thought isn't it? OK. Jeans it is'. She put her black dress back in the cupboard and pulled her jeans on.

'So, are you going to tell me what the occasion is?' said Jenny 'I can't remember the last time you offered to take me out for a drink. It must be something pretty special'.

Julie handed her the promotion letter.

'Read that', she said. 'As from next week I'll be earning a couple of thousand more'.

Jenny scanned the letter. 'Well, the drinks certainly are on you. You should be taking me out for a meal too. You can afford it now'.

'I've already eaten' shrugged Julie. 'Never mind. Maybe another day. Perhaps I'll take you out when I see some of this money. I haven't earnt it yet and I don't have that much to keep me going in the meantime'.

'Oh, my heart bleeds, said Jenny with a laugh. 'You'll soon have plenty spare. Are you ready yet?'

Julie took a last look in the mirror. 'Yep – Just finished. Let's go'.

The Magpie was a popular pub and it was just beginning to get busy when they arrived. They managed to squeeze on the corner of a table filled with teenagers who were busy trying to drink themselves under the table. A couple of them kept glancing over at Julie and Jenny, admiring them, and looking away again if either of the two women turned around. As the night wore on, it became more and more apparent.

'Fancy a toy boy?' said Julie, nodding down towards the youngsters. 'You might be able to teach him a thing or two'. She was on her fourth rum and black, and her voice was a bit louder than it would normally have been.

The boys looked uncomfortable, and Jenny laughed and blew a kiss to the nearest of them. They both went bright red, and looked away quickly, desperately looking for an excuse to leave the table. One of them saw an old friend at the fruit machine and made a beeline for him. The other followed close behind, glancing back quickly to see Julie and Jenny fall about laughing.

Julie hadn't felt so good in a long time. The drinks were relaxing her nicely and she always had fun when she caught up with Jenny. She still hadn't spotted a man that fitted her – in her opinion, quite short list of requirements. She had taken several surreptitious glances around the pub and none of them had appealed to her. She had noticed one of the barmen eyeing Jenny up earlier though.

'What about him? He seems quite nice', she said.

'Which one' replied Jenny, her eyes darting around the pub. 'They all seem fairly gorgeous to me. More so than an hour ago actually. Might be something to do with the wine'. She took another swig of her large glass that was diminishing rapidly.

'The one behind the bar' Julie said laughing. 'He smiled at you when he came around collecting glasses earlier'.

'What him?'. She pointed straight at him. 'The one with the funny eyes?'

Julie chuckled as he looked over at them.

'Did you see his eyes?' continued Jenny in her blaring voice. 'One of them was green, the other one blue. His face looks like a snooker table. He could use his nose as a cue if he wanted to'. She mimed potting a ball with her nose, and nearly knocked the remains of her wine over.

Julie had tears rolling down her eyes from laughing. She finished her drink and went up to the bar to get another one.

'Hi', she said. 'You'll have to excuse my friend. She gets a bit loud when she's had a few drinks'.

'I think you both do', he said with a smile. 'What can I get you?'.

'Ask him for his body' shouted Jenny from the table. Maybe it's soft and green. She was obsessed with her snooker analogy. He laughed.

'It's not for sale' he shouted back. 'How much is yours?'

'Oh priceless' said Jenny joining them at the bar. 'You won't find curves like this going cheap you know'.

Julie got the drinks and took them back to the table, but Jenny had taken quite a shine to the barman. She was feeling a bit left out and by the time Jenny tore herself away and returned to the table. Julie had finished her drink and started on the one she had bought for Jenny. She was becoming very lightheaded.

'Looks like I've got a date for tomorrow night' said Jenny beaming. 'Well spotted. It's a shame we can't find someone for you. We could have a foursome'.

'I could bring one of our little friends' said Julie, indicating the two boys who had been eyeing them up earlier. 'I'll go and ask them'.

Jenny laughed as Julie staggered towards them, nearly toppling over on the way.

'Hi' she said, putting an arm around each of them. 'I'm looking for a date for tomorrow night. Preferably someone rich and handsome'. Her voice was becoming slurred. 'But at the moment, I'm not too fussy because I'm too pissed to tell'.

The two boys looked petrified. They weren't used to women confronting them like this, especially one in Julie's state. Jenny saved them from any further embarrassment.

'Come along Julie' she said, grabbing her friends' arm and pulling her away. 'Time to go home'.

'Let me go' cried Julie. 'I wanted to ask him back to my place'.

'I think he's a bit too young for you'.

'So what. I'm too drunk to notice'. She turned to one of them. 'Do you fancy coming back to my place for a quick...'

'No' shouted Jenny laughing, and dragged her away while she protested at every step.

'I was going to say "drink". For a quick drink'. Julie could barely stand up now. 'Honest I was. I couldn't manage anything else anyway'.

'OK. If you say so'. They had reached the door to the pub.

'Can I drive?' said Julie, tripping down the steps. 'I want to drive. Where's the car?'

'We haven't got a car' said Jenny. 'We got a taxi. Don't you remember?'

'Can I drive the taxi then?'

'No'. Jenny was heading for the phone box outside the pub when a taxi pulled up.

'Are you free?' she called to the driver.

'No luv, I charge like everyone else'.

'I mean. Has anyone booked you?'

He laughed. 'Jump in. Where are you heading?'

Jenny decided it would be best if they went back to her place. She was getting tired now and she didn't think she could cope with getting Julie up to her first floor flat. She gave him the address to her house and settled down in the back.

'Did you ask if I could drive?' mumbled Julie sleepily.

'Shh. Go to sleep' said Jenny. 'I'll wake you when we get there'. It wasn't long before Julie was snoring gently. I hope she doesn't vomit thought Jenny. She didn't want to spoil a good night.

When the taxi pulled up ten minutes later, Julie was still snoring away. She was always like this after a few drinks. Jenny jumped out and paid the driver.

'Can you hang on a mo?' she asked. 'I'll go and get the front door open and come back for her. I'll doubt she'll make it up the steps alone'.

'No problem luv. We're not very busy tonight'.

The driver watched her walk up the path to the small steps. He counted them absently as she climbed them. She fumbled in her bag and pulled out a small bundle of keys, opened the front door and turned on the light. When she was out of sight, the driver hit the accelerator and screeched down the road at high speed. Glancing in his rear-view mirror he saw Jenny running down the garden path shouting after him.

Julie slept on in the back as the taxi sped off down the road, turned a corner and disappeared into the night.

Chapter 10 – "The Pond"

'Good morning Mr McDonald. I trust you slept well. Your breakfast awaits you'.

Zak sat up on the bed and rubbed his eyes. He was pleased to find that his headache had cleared and that his body didn't ache as much as he thought it would after his heavy meetings with the floor yesterday. The lights had been switched back on and the bed had been raised to the hole for him. He stumbled through it and made his way to the sink in the kitchen. A towel had been left out for him and he had a quick wash before settling down for breakfast.

Breakfast was a little better than his evening meal – but not much. It consisted of a bowl of cereal, that could have been cornflakes, but he couldn't really tell due to their lack of taste. There were also two eggs – which were a little more edible. I suppose it's difficult to get eggs wrong, he thought. He had a good sniff of the food before eating it, looking for any traces of – well, something out of the ordinary.

'Don't worry Mr McDonald. Your food hasn't been tampered with today. As I told you last night we want to keep your strength up'.

Zak decided to eat the food whatever it might contain. If they wanted to kill him, they would have done it long ago.

'Are you going to tell me what exciting things you've got in store for me today?' he said between mouthfuls of egg. 'If it's anything like yesterday, I think I'll pass and go back to bed for a couple more hours'.

'You must stop being so negative. Didn't I tell you to treat this place like a holiday camp? First things first. I haven't introduced myself yet. That was a bit rude of me. My name is Ronald Miller. You can call me Ron'.

'I'd rather call you shithead' said Zak angrily. Ron continued as if he hadn't spoken.

'You don't mind if I call you by your first name, do you? Mr McDonald seems far too formal. It's Zak isn't it?'

Zak ignored him and helped himself to a glass of water from the tap.

'Yes, Zak. When you have finished your breakfast, you can make your way to the bathroom. I'm sure you would appreciate a shower before....'.

Zak cut him off. 'Before what? Before I go insane from hearing you droning on? Before I get thrown in another room in the dark and nearly kill myself? I'm not taking any more orders from you until you tell me why the hell I'm here and what you want from me. Until then, I'm just going to keep looking for a way out. I did pretty well yesterday. I'm sure I can find a way out of this room just as easily'.

'I'm sure you can Zak. Have you tried the door? I thought not. You might find things a little different today. I don't want to be enemies with you. As long as you cooperate, then we'll get along fine. I told you yesterday that no harm would come to you. That's only true if you help me out and do as you're told. Is that asking too much?'

Zak walked to the door and opened it. The brick wall had gone. Puzzled, he walked through the door and found himself in a bathroom.

The bathroom was neatly decorated and tiled from floor to ceiling around the bath and sink. There was a normal, proper functioning toilet too. No hole in the ground. No strange buttons to operate it. Just a toilet. Zak took a look around before stripping and having a long, hot shower. He couldn't see a camera in this room. At least he had a bit of privacy. Above the door, raised vertically upwards it seemed, was the brick wall that had blocked his path the day before. It seemed that everything around him was being controlled remotely. He wouldn't be surprised if his breakfast had been dropped from a hole in the ceiling. He didn't think anyone would have risked coming in and setting it out neatly while he had slept close by.

He towel-dried himself, dressed again and returned to the kitchen.

'OK shithead', he said. 'Are you going to show me the way out of here or do I have to spend hours searching again?'

'Ah Zak. I hope you feel better after your shower. Please – take a seat'.

As he spoke, a small partition at the far end of the kitchen started to revolve, revealing a chair from the other side of the wall. So that's how I got in here, he thought. He had a quick look around to see if there was anything else he wanted to take. Other than the few items he had grabbed yesterday the only thing that seemed useful was the rope from the larder. He grabbed it and coiled it around his neck so his hands were free, and cautiously sat in the chair. Nothing happened for a moment, and he was about to get up again when the chair slowly rotated around, leaving the kitchen behind him.

****

Julie knew she wasn't at home the moment she opened her eyes. The room was far too big and luxurious – nothing like her tiny flat. She sat up with a gasp and looked around.

She was in a magnificently decorated bedroom. There were several expensive looking pictures on the wall, beautiful velvet lined curtains at the windows and a carpet with a pile so deep that her feet almost disappeared when she stood up on it. The bed she had slept in was a four poster with silk sheets and satin pillowcases. One of the walls at the far end of the room was completely mirrored. It wasn't covered in lots of small, tacky mirrored tiles, but just one very large floor to ceiling, wall to wall mirror – around fifteen-foot square.

She was also very aware that her clothes were gone, and she was in her underwear.

'Jenny?' she called, and then again a little more urgently 'Jenny? Where are you? Where are we?'

There was no reply. She got up, wrapping the plush duvet around her and walked slowly around the room, trying to remember the night before. Her head was pounding, and memories from the Magpie the night before came flooding back. OK, so she had had a few drinks, but how on Earth had she ended up here? Had Jenny set her up with a millionaire when she was too far gone to remember? No such luck. It was more likely to be a practical joke.

She found a glass of water with two paracetamol on the side of a solid wood dressing table which she swallowed gratefully. A door led to an en-suite bathroom which was decorated in the same lavish manner.

She called out again, but it seemed that she was alone.

Locking the bathroom door, she stripped and stepped into the shower and turned on the water. Whoever brought her here wouldn't mind if she had a quick shower she decided. She felt she needed one. There was a strong stench of cigarette smoke about her after spending the evening in the pub. As she stood there enjoying the hot soapy water streaming down her naked body, she racked her brain to try and remember what had happened. She could remember Jenny chatting up the bloke at the bar. Quite cute. Snooker-ball eyes. Perhaps this was his place and they had all come back for a nightcap.

She jumped out of the shower and wrapped a heavy, soft towel around her that she found on a heated towel rail and dried herself quickly. Well, whoever's house I'm in isn't short of a bob or two, she thought. Could a barman afford something like this?

She found her clothes washed, ironed and neatly hung up in the huge mahogany wardrobe opposite the bed. After dressing, she opened the curtains and found some patio doors with a stunning view. She opened them and stepped out.

There was a wide expanse of green fields on her left, but it was the view in front of her at the end of the garden that took her breath away. There were some steps leading down to a beautiful, deserted sandy beach. The sea was so calm, that it was hardly moving. If it wasn't for the sand, she would have mistaken if for a giant lake. There was no movement in the trees, and the sun shone brightly spilling light over Julie and into the bedroom. Between her and the beach, there was a magnificent pond, taking up most of the garden, with a cute wooden bridge running across it, just in front of where Julie was standing. She stepped onto it and looked around again in awe. The pond must have been about sixty foot in diameter and surrounded by plants and shrubs of brilliant shapes and colours. An old oak tree hung over one end of the pond, it's almost perfect reflection reaching towards her in the still water. She heard the sound of running water and noticed a small river trickling down towards the sea.

It was perfect. She could have stood on the bridge all day, just looking at the array of beautiful sights. Every time she looked around; she saw something that she had missed before. An incredibly realistic ornamental duck on one side of the pond. A tiny island in the middle of the pond with a circle of bored looking gnomes fishing over the side. There wasn't a cloud in sight. She walked across the bridge, facing the sea and took it all in.

It was all so still. No movement. No people. No birds. That's a bit odd, she thought. Why is it so deserted on such a lovely day? Why isn't there anybody at all? What am I doing at the beach? Her mind was racing again, and this last thought hung in her mind. Last night she was in a pub that stood about forty odd miles from the nearest coastline. What was she doing by the sea?

She turned back to the house and noticed it for the first time. She had been so overwhelmed with the glorious garden that she hadn't bothered to look behind her. The house wasn't a house at all. It was just a room. Two rooms if you counted the bathroom she had showered in. It was more like a giant beach hut. Behind it was a high wall, masked by trees that looked over the hut. There wasn't even a proper door. Just the patio doors that she had come through. The image of the perfect house faded immediately. She went back into the "house" puzzled. Why wasn't there a kitchen? Such a stunning place couldn't really be used if it was only a bedroom and bathroom. Why was there nobody else here? She had assumed that whoever had brought her here was sleeping somewhere else in the house, but now it was clear she was alone.

    She decided she had to find someone and work out where she was. She pulled the patio doors closed and set off for the beach. Despite her predicament, she found that the magnificent bedroom and garden had lifted her spirits. Her headache had almost gone too, and as she walked, she found herself singing softly. Not a bad way to spend a Sunday, wherever I am she thought.

Chapter 11 – "Humbug"

Zak got off the chair and scanned the room. It was the size of a sports hall but with a low ceiling. Very low. Zak's head only fell a few inches short of it. If he had jumped too high, he would have had another bump to add to his increasing list of bruises. The other odd thing about the ceiling was that it was made completely of glass.

As he stared, a fish dived downwards toward him, catching him by surprise and making him duck. The fish opened and closed its mouth frantically making it look like it was arguing about something. Zak recovered his composure at the sounds of Ron's laughter.

'Do you like my fish tank? I like to be different you know. It's kind of a hobby of mine. The fish that is. Not the "being different". They're such wonderful creatures. I can sit and watch them for hours, just swimming up and down – not a care in the world. It's very relaxing. Watching fish. Calms the nerves, or so my doctor once told me. Perhaps you should take his advice too and spend a few hours here. You've been a little troubled lately'.

There was a mocking tone to Ron's voice that Zak chose to ignore. 'I think I'll pass. I'd rather find my way out of here' he said, looking around. 'I can't see a door in here either. I don't suppose for a second it would have a handle or anything obvious like that?'

'But I brought you here for recreation' said Ron. 'I'm offended now. I bring you here to have a game with you and all you can do is talk about getting out'.

'Well, if you're so keen on playing then why don't you join me?' said Zak. 'I'm fed up hearing your annoying voice when I can't see who it belongs to. Come down here and I'll show you a game or two'. His voice was rising, and he turned in circles looking around his as he spoke, trying to spot the camera he was being watched by.

'I think I'll play from here' said Ron. I believe you picked up a gun from the larder yesterday. I suggest you get hold of it quickly. I think you're going to need it'.

As Ron finished speaking, Zak noticed the chair turning back into the wall that he had come from, closing off the space between the two rooms. He heard a click and the lights dimmed until a faint glow from the water above was the only light in the room. He could see fairly well from it, but the movement in the water above cast strange shadows around the room producing a very eerie unnerving effect

'Here we go again' shouted Zak. 'Let's just turn out all the lights so I can't see properly. Very original. So what happens next? Are the fish gonna dance for me?'

The only answer that Zak got was another click that sounded like it came from the far wall. A yellow light emerged in the air and started travelling towards him, slowly at first, but picking up speed as it got nearer. It was about the size of a football but had the shape of a bird. The bird flew closer and the light changed to a bright red colour, illuminating the bird so Zak could see it clearly.

It looks like a bird, thought Zak. But it can't be because it's got a light up its backside. Then he noticed the top was spinning like a helicopter. OK, so it's a remote-controlled plane. Sounds about right for this place. Everything else is remote controlled. The front of the bird had two large glass eyes that were staring straight at Zak's head. On the underside was a piece of glass that must have been a bulb as it was here that the light was coming from.

As Zak was taking all of this in, he suddenly realized that the bird, or whatever it was, had no intention of stopping. It was coming at him fast. Closer.

And Closer.

He ducked. The bird whisked over his head, falling slightly to follow Zak's movement, but not quite enough to collide with his head. He felt the wind rush as it passed him, swooping upwards again, and dropping something from its rear end as it did so. Zak was still watching as it expertly straightened up, just missing the glass roof, turned in a wide arc and headed back down the room to where it had come from. As it flew off, the colour changed back to yellow.

The glass ball that the bird had dropped hit the ground in front of Zak and exploded into a puff of colourful smoke. He gasped in shock and the gasp turned into a choke as the smoke caught in his lungs. He staggered away from the smoke just in time to see the bird turn around and come back for another try. As it came nearer, Zak's eyes began to water from the aftereffects of the smoke. He could barely see as the bird homed in on him again.

When it was fairly close, he threw himself to the ground, hoping that he had judged it just right. The bird swooped down, even closer than before, but again just missed. Another glass ball dropped from it and Zak found himself smothered in the dense smoke again. He scrambled away to fresh air, and remembering Ron's last words, fumbled for the gun in his pocket. He pulled out the fork first and tossed it aside angrily. He glanced up and saw the bird had turned again and was on its way back. Keeping one eye on the bird, he felt around in his pocket again, this time pulling out the strange gun. He didn't know what effect it would have but pointed it at the bird anyway.

The threat of the gun didn't deter the bird in any way. It kept on coming, the light bobbing up and down slightly. Zak pulled the trigger and saw the gun's beam of light appear just above the bird's head. He lowered his aim slightly, tracking the bird as he did, and caught the tip of the bird – but it kept coming. Suddenly, the light on the underside of the bird turned to red and it seemed to pick up speed as it made a beeline for him. Zak stood his ground and lowered the gun just a touch more. He had tears streaming down his face from his watering eyes, and his heart was hammering when he hit the bird between the eyes. It was only a few feet away and he had to duck again as it exploded in a ball of flame and dive bombed to the ground at the side of him. On impact, the small glass bomb shattered too, releasing more of the suffocating smoke.

'Jesus Christ' he shouted, as he staggered away again and collapsed against the wall until his breathing returned to normal.

When most of the smoke had dissipated, he went over to look at the remains of the bird. It was a mess. Lots of circuitry, motors and smouldering, broken pieces of plastic were scattered around. It had well and truly been destroyed. He kicked the pile of rubble and headed up towards the end of the room that the bird had come from, gun still in has hand just in case he should be attacked again. There was a hole in the wall, about chest level, a foot square, just big enough for the bird but not quite big enough for Zak. He stuck his head into it and shone the light from the gun inside, but there was nothing to see. He shouted into the hole.

'What's the big idea Ron? You don't impress me with your little games. It all seems like a waste of time to me. What have you really got me here for?'

He didn't get a reply. His voice echoed around the room and then there was silence. He sank to the floor where he was and ran his fingers through his hair. There must be a way out he thought. This place can't be completely secure. It's too big. He stood up and made his way around the walls, repeating the steps he had done last night in the bedroom, examining them for the first time. It was becoming a bit of a bind, scrutinising every wall that he came across. He knew that most things here were operated remotely, but if he kept checking he might get lucky.

As he reached the third wall, a section of it slid across in front of him, revealing a further room. He nearly didn't go through as he felt he was being led around the complex like a dog on a chain. In the end he decided that he had nothing better to do and stepped into the new room. The wall slid silently into place behind him.

****

Julie walked leisurely along the beach basking in the glorious sun. She hadn't come across anyone yet and she thought it was a bit strange. Her watch told her that it was nearly eleven o'clock. Surely somebody would be up and about. As she walked, she remembered the last time she had walked along a deserted beach like this. She hadn't realised that it had been so long ago. The beach was always swarming with people when she went to the seaside and it had been nearly ten years since she had seen one empty like this.

She had been nineteen and in love with a student named Liam, and they had taken a drive to the beach in Liam's Ford Capri one night at 3am. How young and foolish she had been then. She had thought that Liam was the most perfect man in the world and could do no wrong. She always did what he wanted and didn't argue when he didn't want to do what she did. She trusted him when he told her he was going out with the lads and it took her months to realise he was seeing that slag Libby Baxter behind her back. It had taken her a long time to get over the humiliation and now she smiled as she recollected the past. Lucky escape. I wonder what happened to him, she thought. He probably ended up in journalism like he always wanted to, or Libby might have got pregnant and he was probably tied to her now. Serve him right, she mused.

She left the beach and headed towards a row of shops that ran alongside. As she approached, she saw movement in one of the shop entrances. It was a dog. A small black and grey scottie dog.

'Hello boy' she said, crouching down and holding her hand out towards it. The dog sniffed her fingers cautiously and then, deciding she was friendly, licked them and wagged its tail. It was awfully thin and covered in dirt. Must be a stray, she thought. He was wearing a collar with a tag though, but it didn't give an address or phone number. Just his name – "Humbug". She stood up and looked into the shop but couldn't see anybody.

'Stay here Humbug. I'll only be gone a minute'.

The dog looked at her incomprehensibly but sat down as she entered the shop.

'Hello?' she called stepping into the tiny shop. 'Anybody here?'

It was a gift shop stocked with all the usual "tat" found in a seaside gift shop. Postcards, sticks of rock, keyrings, cheap bathing costumes, rubber rings, beach hats, buckets and spades. Every shelf was overflowing with useless beach treasures that always ended up in the junk cupboard a couple of days after returning home. There was no one in the shop though despite the sign saying it was "OPEN". There wasn't even a back room or storeroom that she could see. Just a few shelves and a till which was powered off. The only sign of anybody being there recently was the fact that the shop was open.

She returned to the dog who was still sitting patiently outside.

'Looks like there's nobody here' she said to Humbug. 'Where did you come from? You're the only sign of life I've seen all day'.

She looked up and down the beach, but it was still deserted. She started off again with her new-found friend skipping at her heels.

****

An hour later, Julie still hadn't found anyone, and panic had begun to set in. She had left the beach and followed a side street into a busy shopping precinct.

Except it wasn't busy.

On any other weekend day, it would have been filled with bustling shoppers and beachgoers on the hunt for bargains, pushing their way through the crowds, arguing with one another about how much prices had risen and how their money didn't seem to last as long anymore. There was a road running through which should have been end to end with cars looking for places to park, stereos blaring through the open windows with impatient drivers complaining about the heat.

The whole place was like a graveyard though.

Humbug had stayed with her on the long walk and he was beginning to flag. His tongue was hanging out as he panted at her feet and he began to whine.

'Getting thirsty boy?' she said kneeling down, petting the tired dog. She was glad of his company. If she'd been completely on her own, she would have gone mad by now. 'I'll see if I can find a drink'.

She could do with a drink herself, so headed to a small newsagent and tried the door. To her astonishment it opened. It was only then that she realised that all the shops were open. All the lights in the stores were lit, and some even had their doors propped open. She was amazed that she hadn't noticed before. She helped herself to a couple of cans of cola and a bottle of water, and as an afterthought grabbed some crisps and chocolate. She hadn't eaten all day and the sight of the chocolate began to make her mouth water. She opened her purse and left some money on the counter. Not that anybody would have seen her. She could have ransacked the whole shop and burnt it to the ground without anyone being aware. She left the money as it had seemed like the right thing to do. She realised after that she had done it in a bid to convince herself that nothing was wrong. That the shop owner had just popped out for a couple of minutes and taken everyone with him. They would all be back soon, laughing and joking about.

Her thoughts were distracted as she saw movement in the distance at the other end of the long street. Even Humbug had pricked his ears up and was looking that way. She quickly poured some water in a puddle for the dog which he lapped up gratefully, and then hurried down towards…..towards what? What exactly had she seen? Just a flash of colour. A movement in the shadows. If it had been a windy day, she may have dismissed as a trick of the light, but the desperation and isolation had convinced her that it was something more. She hadn't seen any movement since she had left the beach with its rising and falling waves.

Suddenly, she saw it again. She hadn't imagined it. It looked like a child. A young girl on roller skates gliding along the road as if nothing was wrong. She turned a corner in the distance and vanished.

'Wait' cried Julie running after her, the dog at her heels. Yapping excitedly. 'Please wait'.

She dashed up the road to the turning that the girl had taken, just in time to see her turn into another side street further up. She followed as quickly as she could, her feet now aching from the long walk and desperate run up the street. As she rounded the next corner, she came to an abrupt halt and her eyes opened wide.

There was nobody around to hear her scream.

Chapter 12 - "Rabbits"

'I'm impressed Mr McDonald'.

'Oh, so you're back. I thought you'd forgotten all about me', replied Zak sarcastically. 'I must say. I did enjoy that. What other exciting activities have you got lined up for me? I've always fancied a bit of snorkelling. Perhaps I can practice in your fish tank'.

The fish still swam above his head. It seemed that the tank covered more than just one room. The same dull glow came from above lighting the room dimly for him.

It was another round room with, what looked like a thin running track around the perimeter. The track spiralled inwards though towards a small platform in the centre of the room that contained a chair.

'I'm sorry. Snorkelling's not on the agenda for today' said Ron with a chuckle. 'I'll see what I can do though. We might be able to squeeze you in for a session next week'.

'No good Ron. I'll be out of here by then. Looks like I'll have to miss out on it'. Zak walked to the centre of the room and examined the chair. It was bolted down to the platform, which rotated in a full circle when he moved it. He sat down and scanned the room as he spun in the chair.

'Well, if you insist. Snorkelling isn't much fun anyway. You'll prefer this I think'.

'I can't wait' mumbled Zak.

Ron's laughter echoed around the room and Zak nearly fell of the chair as it began to rotate on its own accord. It wasn't too fast, but he began to get dizzy after a while. He was about to get up when he heard a click and two leg cuffs appeared from the chair legs and locked around his ankles, pinning him to the chair.

'Hey'.

He heard three high pitched beeps followed by another even higher. At the last one. A trap opened at one of the walls and a rabbit shot along the track at high speed.

Zak looked at it in amazement. It's like a mini a greyhound track, he thought. But without the dogs. Why would this be here?

The small electronic rabbit continued to dash around the track. It appeared to be self-powered and had wheels which were guided by the edges of the track. A light shone brightly from it and a small round target was painted in bright colours on its side. After a couple of revolutions, Zak noticed it was getting closer. It was following the spiralling track to the point where he sat. It took him two more revolutions before he saw the small glass bomb attached to the front of the rabbit.

Here we go again.

He fumbled for the gun again and took aim. His chair was rotating in the opposite direction to that of the rabbit making life very difficult for him. As it came closer, he swung around in the chair, not taking his eyes off the fast approaching mammal. He squeezed the trigger and watched the beam duck and dive around it. He was beginning to feel sick with the constant spinning, and his aim was a long way off.

As the rabbit got nearer and the spirals got shorter – the rabbit appeared to be moving faster. It was almost on top of him when he started to panic. He thrashed around in the chair trying to break out of the ankle cuffs, but they held strong. The rabbit was just feet away. Zak leaned forward and in one deft move plucked the rabbit from the track and took the glass ball off it.

Immediately, another rabbit shot on to the track at the edge of the room. He watched it for a few seconds, then put the first rabbit back on the track in the wrong direction. He watched the two rabbits hurtle towards each other at a suicidal rate.

The explosion that followed the collision caused both rabbits to leap into the air like fireworks. One of them smashed onto the low ceiling and disintegrated. Zak heard a small click and noticed that one of the cuffs had retracted. One kill, one cuff he mused.

The other rabbit flew straight towards Zak like a fireball. He threw himself down as far as the other ankle cuff would allow and the flaming rabbit just missed him, clipped the top of his chair and broke apart.

Click. He was free.

He stood up, breathing heavily, and examined the small glass ball he had taken from the rabbit, glad that he hadn't broken it. The smoke earlier had almost choked him. He threw it as far away as possible and it shattered against the wall. The smoke he was expecting didn't come. Instead it exploded with a loud bang, knocking a hole in the wall it had hit. Zak's mouth fell open in astonishment. If that had hit the chair it would have blown his leg off. He felt his knees go weak and fell to the ground shaking as a third rabbit was released onto the track.

'OK. That's enough' he screamed. 'What the hell are you playing at you bastard? Are you trying to kill me?'

The rabbit dashed towards him and he scrambled to his feet as it narrowly passed by his head. He went to the edge of the room and peered through the hole that the tiny bomb had made. All he could see was a long corridor with a door at the end. The corridor was empty, and he couldn't get through the hole anyway.

He turned back and watched the rabbit getting closer to the chair. He glanced back at the hole in the wall and had an idea. The rabbit was nearly at the centre so he would have to be quick. He dashed back towards the chair and stood over it as the rabbit passed him. Three more revolutions to go. Two. His heart was pounding as he grabbed at the rabbit on its last revolution. He nearly missed. His fingers slipped at first and just caught the back of it lifting it free from the track. The small glass bomb on the front got dislodged. Almost in slow motion, Zak screamed and threw himself to the ground to catch it. He made it by three inches and scooped it up in relief.

He lay there for a few seconds catching his breath, glass bomb in one hand, rabbit in the other – wheels still spinning at high speed. He stood up, being extra careful with the small bomb and headed to the hole in the wall. Now he knew what the glass ball was capable of, he treated it with more respect. He carefully balanced the bomb on the wall where the gap was and stood back. He braced himself and threw the rabbit at the bomb, ducking down in anticipation of the blast.

It didn't come. He'd missed, and by an unlucky twist of fate, the rabbit landed on its wheels and headed up the track. He groaned as it shot back into its trap and disappeared. He rolled over and lay on the ground, sighing heavily. The light shone down from the fish tank above, shimmering as the various fish swam by. I'm under the tank, he thought. Which means – there has to be a top to it.

A sudden fit of anger overtook him. He'd had enough. He'd been cooped up for ages, nearly choked to death, and narrowly missed being killed by an exploding rabbit. He jumped to his feet, retrieved the glass bomb and raised it over his head. There was a second's hesitation as the rational side of his brain told him not to do it, but he ignored the logical reasoning and tossed the bomb at the glass ceiling.

As the bomb exploded, he almost regretted doing it. He dived for cover as gallons of water began to flood in.

****

Julie staggered back gasping and was violently sick up the wall by her side. She kept on heaving until there was nothing left to come up. She sank to her knees trying to catch her breath as the pain in her stomach subsided. When she had recovered slightly, she took a sideways glance back towards the girl on the skates.

She was impaled in the middle of a large sheet of glass that ran across the length of the road about twenty feet in front of her. As Julie had turned the corner, she had seen the whole horrific accident happen as if it were a video playing in slow motion. If only she could have paused it, stopping the action before the girl could skate straight into the glass. Before the flying splinters could tear away shreds of flesh from the girls' face and arms. Before she had fallen on the razor-sharp points that still remained in the pane of glass. The girl lay limply in a spreading pool of her own blood, not breathing. It had killed her instantly.

Humbug had wandered over and was sniffing around at the lacerated body. As Julie watched in horror, he licked at the blood trickling down the girl's arm.

'No', she screamed jumping up and running towards the small dog. She reached down to pluck him off the ground but slipped on the blood and fell awkwardly landing on the girl's body. If the girl hadn't died from the impact with the glass, the extra weight pushing her further onto the spikes of glass would certainly have finished her off. Fresh blood oozed from these deeper wounds, covering Julie's hands as she scrambled to her feet screaming.

She ran around the corner and bolted down the street hysterically, Humbug at her feet. She didn't stop running until her body decided it couldn't go any further. She fell to the ground, exhausted, shaking and sobbing. The image of the young girl came flooding back and Julie's world faded away as she lost consciousness.

Chapter 13 – "Escape"

Zak scrambled to the side of the room as he was showered with water and fish. He hadn't expected the bomb to make such a large hole, and the force of the downpour was causing it to become bigger. There was a growing stream of water appearing on the floor, filling the track that the rabbit had run along, helping some of the smaller fish to survive.

An alarm started wailing nearby and he heard footsteps approaching fast from up the corridor. He peered through the hole in the wall and saw three armed guards running towards him. He watched as they got closer thinking that the door must be in this wall somewhere. He splashed away from the guards and concealed himself behind the waterfall that was coming from above. It had no indication of slowing down, and he found himself paddling in a several inches of rising water. He didn't hear the door slide open over the sounds of the running water, but he knew they were there as the level dropped slightly as water escaped into the corridor. He held his breath and put his head through the downpour to get an idea of where they were.

He saw them just as they began to separate, one going to the left, one to right. The third one stood guarding the door, looking around trying to spot him. At one point, he stared directly at Zak, but then looked away. With all the water, and fish dropping from above, Zak was completely obscured.

He had an idea. The revolving chair was next to him on the hidden side of the waterfall, occupied by a large fish that was wriggling in a vain attempt to get some water into its gills. Zak obliged, knocking it into the stream. He stood on the chair, and taking a deep breath, plunged his head through the hole in the ceiling. His hands grabbed the sides of the hole and he half pushed, half dragged himself out of the round room and into the fish tank above. His head broke the surface and he gasped for breath. He found he could stand up in the tank with his head out of the water.

He had hoped that he would be able to swim through the massive tank to an entry point. The fish had to be fed from somewhere. He hadn't expected to find himself looking out over a huge garden from an equally huge pond. He blinked in disbelief but realised he didn't have time to waste. He swam to the side of the pond and hoisted himself out, glad that there was nobody to witness his strange entry into the outside world. He watched the water disappearing from the pond for a second more. It was as if someone had just removed the plug from a giant bath, the water spiralling towards the hole from which he had emerged.

He decided to get as far away as possible before the guards realised where he had gone. He headed towards the beach, the hot sun drying his clothes as he ran away from the underground complex. He was glad to be back in the fresh air.

****

'What do you mean gone?' Ron was having trouble trying to comprehend why three armed men couldn't apprehend one unarmed one who was trapped in a room. It didn't make sense to him. He had discovered that Zak had his wits about him, but it should have taken far more than that to get past his guards.

'He wasn't there sir. We checked the whole room. The only way he could have got out was through the roof. Through the hole that he'd made.'

Ron sat down and flicked a couple of switches on the panel in front of him. The screen showed him a view of the large pond that wasn't really a pond any more. The water had all flooded into the room below, leaving a few dead fish and pond weeds. The hole in the bottom could clearly be seen from this angle and Ron cursed aloud when he saw the extent of the damage. He punched a button and flicked between the different cameras on the site. He hesitated when he came to the view of the young roller skater embedded in the pane of glass.

He grabbed a phone and tapped a number in.

'Morning John. There's a broken pane in sector twelve. Can you get one of your lads on to it? You'll need a body bag too. One of our guests has had an unfortunate accident. Oh, and try and keep it as discrete as possible. There's a new arrival loose on site'.

He put the phone down and turned back to the monitor. A few screens later he came across Julie slumped on the ground in the shopping centre. He smiled and pressed another button causing another screen to blink into life with the same image.

'Watch that screen', he said to one of the guards. 'Tell me if she moves. I want to keep an eye on her'. He flicked between the remaining cameras but couldn't find Zak.

'Little shit's hiding. Find him. I want him under complete surveillance. Do what you have you. I want him bugged if possible. There's no use bringing him back in now'.

Two of the guards left promptly leaving Ron with the third, who was watching Julie on the small screen.

'He shouldn't have got out yet', said Ron to himself. 'We should have watched him closer'.

He turned back to his screen and began scanning the complex again.

****

The sun was high in the sky when Julie came around and it took her a while to realise where she was. She slowly got to her feet and her muscles screamed in pain from sleeping on the hard pavement. How long had she been out? Was it minutes? Hours? Humbug had been curled up at her feet dozing, and he woke too when she stirred. She was petting the dog, pleased that he'd stayed with her when she spotted the blood stains on her hands.

Everything came flooding back like a bad dream.

The young girl.

The glass.

The squishing sound that came from the dead body when she'd slipped and fell on it.

She shivered and looked over her shoulder as if she expected the mangled corpse to be around, stalking her. Should she go back? She was a witness. Someone would want to know what happened. But who? Seeing the girl had proved that there were other people around, but she'd been the only one all day. And she was dead now.

She toyed with the idea of going back and trying to find someone, but the memories of the blood and the girl's lifeless eyes put her off the idea. It was obvious what had happened, she thought. No one needs me to point it out.

It was a pretty feeble excuse and she knew it, but once her mind was made up she knew she wouldn't go back. Her first priority was to the wash the blood off her hands. She found a chemist nearby that had a staff washroom at the back. There was nobody there, so she helped herself to soap and spent five minutes thoroughly scrubbing her hands under the hot water. When she was satisfied that her hands were blood free, she stripped off her top and splashed water on her face and under her arms. Feeling much better, she dressed and returned to the high street.

What now? she thought looking up and down the empty row of shops. She had almost become accustomed to the idea that there was no one around. It was beginning to seem normal that all the shops were open but completely empty. But where was everyone?

She picked a direction at random and followed it, hoping that it would lead to something that might make sense of it all. She was so preoccupied with the strange town and what might have happened to all the people, that she nearly walked straight past the phone box. She kicked herself for not thinking of it before and opened the door.

Picking up the receiver she knew it was going to be dead and was startled when she got a tone. She quickly dialled her mother's number and waited, holding her breath in anticipation. After fifteen rings, she hung up and tried again. She let it ring for a whole two minutes this time before putting the phone back in the cradle in dismay. Her mother was always in. The phone couldn't have been working properly. She tried Jenny, and then a couple more numbers but got the same result. She was about to leave, when she saw the sign on the phone.

"Dial 999 for emergencies. You will not be charged for these calls".

She let the door fall shut again and reached for the "9". After just two rings, there was a click and a man spoke to her.

'Emergency. Which service do you require?'

'Oh. Oh, thank God'. She couldn't believe it. 'I'm calling from a phone box in a shopping centre. I don't know where it is, but…..but there's nobody here. I mean – the whole place is just deserted. Well, almost deserted. I saw a little girl and she was….'.

Julie stopped as the voice at the other end gave a deep chuckle. She began to panic as the laughing got louder and the hairs on the back of her neck stood on end when the voice spoke menacingly to her again'.

'Don't worry Julie. I'll look after you. I won't let any harm come to you'. The man started cackling again and Julie fled from the phone box screaming. The laughter continued to emanate from the receiver like a voice from the grave as it swung back and forth from its curly cable.

Julie never heard it though. She was a long way down the road and getting further away by the second.

****

Ron hung up grinning as he watched her flee from the phone box. He couldn't play with Zak anymore, so having some fun with Julie seemed like the next best thing. She was an easy target. It wouldn't take much to send her over the edge into hysterics. He followed her path with the cameras and saw that she had inadvertently headed back to the beach. He watched her sit on a bench overlooking the long stretch of golden sand and take several nervous glances over her shoulder.

The dog jumped onto the bench and snuggled up next to her, trying to comfort her, sensing she wasn't happy.

At least he had eyes on her. He'd be a bit more relaxed when they found Zak again. He didn't like him wandering around where he couldn't see him. He flicked to another camera and saw a troop of his guards emerging from the garden by the remains of the pond. A voice crackled from the radio at his side.

'No sign of him yet sir. We'll head down to the beach and check the surrounding areas'.

'No. Don't go near the beach. I don't want the girl to see you. Try the park first. I'll try and get her to move'. Ron put the radio down and turned his attention back to Julie.

'Sorry my dear. I'm going to have to move you', he said, stroking Julie's face on the screen. 'I want to use the beach'.

Chapter 14 - "Floop"

Julie was still shaking. It wasn't just the mocking laughter that had given her the shivers. It was what the man had said. He had spoken her name. He knew her. Was he watching her? The worst part was not knowing what was going on, not knowing how she got here. She cuddled the small dog, trying to get some comfort from it but not succeeding. She tried to calm down and think rationally. She wasn't normally such a basket case. Seeing the dead girl had shook her up more than she realised - hardly surprising really. It wasn't the sort of thing she saw every day.

She had tried to put the event to the back of her mind, but now it crept forward. What was the piece of glass doing across the road like that? It wasn't as if it had just been left lying around. It stretched across the whole road, blocking the way through. A solid wall of glass.

And what about the girl? The only person she had seen all day had killed herself in a freak accident. Or had the man on the phone caused it somehow? It didn't seem possible. He might have put the piece of glass up, but he wouldn't be able to persuade her to skate into it. No – it must have just been bad luck. She cringed as the memory started to form in her mind again and quickly pushed it back. She tried to think of happier things to take her mind off it.

The night before, in the pub.

Her promotion.

Even the guy on the platform seemed amusing now. Her mood lifted slightly, and she managed a small smile.

She gazed over the gorgeous beach and relaxed even more. Right – No more hysterics, she thought. Just calm, rational ideas so I can work out what's going on.

Suddenly she heard a rumble. It was quiet at first and quite distant, but it got louder as it got closer. At first, she thought it was coming from further up the beach and she gazed down towards it, shielding her eyes from the sun to see what was causing it. Humbug, who had been growling, stood up on the bench and started barking incessantly but Julie couldn't see a thing. The rumble grew increasingly louder and she realised it was coming from underground. It got closer still, until it sounded as if it was directly below her. Humbug was going berserk, barking at the empty space on the beach where the noise was coming from. Suddenly it stopped. Completely. The silence would have been deafening if it wasn't for the dog.

'It's OK. Calm down', said Julie soothingly, picking him up. 'Whatever it was, it's stopped now'.

The dog stopped barking but still growled uneasily.

'That's better. It's alright'. She stroked him behind the ears, but he wouldn't stop.

Suddenly, something exploded out of the sand, showering her with bits of beach. She screamed, more in surprise than alarm, and turned away to shield her face from the flying sand, dropping the dog as she did so. She turned back to see what it was but there was nothing there. There was a small crater about the size of a dustbin lid in the sand, but there was nothing in it. She noticed that Humbug was barking again but was now looking up. She followed his gaze, and saw a balloon floating a couple of foot above her head. It was a bit bigger than a normal balloon and was making a strange humming noise. She watched in uneasily as it bobbed around above her, not floating away in the wind like a normal balloon would but holding its position.

She got up and took a step away from the bench, and the balloon followed. She walked this way and that but couldn't shake it off. It just stayed above her head, as if it were attached by invisible wires. She stood on the bench, but it rose as she did, staying just above her. She reached up and made a grab for it and it burst showering her with water.

She shrieked in surprise and shook her head to remove the water from her ears, just as another balloon shot out of the ground, showering her in sand again. The second one took up its position above her head and waited. She was puzzled. What was the point? She watched the balloon for a couple of minutes, but it didn't do anything except float around above her. She ran across the road as fast as she could, but it followed her, never far behind.

Five minutes passed, and it still hung there. It was a strange sensation having it floating above her head. She kept looking at it, expecting it to do something, but it never did. She knew what would happen if she touched it, but eventually couldn't help herself. She was driven by the same impulse that made her touch anything that had a "Wet Paint" sign on it – you know, just to see if it was dry.

She reached up cautiously, and just as her fingers touched it, it burst. This time, the water was icy cold, and she squealed again as it ran down her neck.

Floop

A third balloon. A third sand shower. This one didn't hang about. It flew straight at her and burst releasing a ball of smoke. She staggered away coughing as another one appeared. More smoke.

Then cold water.

It had been fairly amusing at first – a practical joke almost, but now she was getting fed up. She headed away from the beach, the dog at her heels and the latest balloon homing in. This one contained cold custard and she screamed in disgust as it trickled down her face. She quickened her pace. If they were going to keep on coming, she would be better off away from the strange crater on the beach where they emerged.

After two more showers, she popped in a gift shop and picked up a large sun hat. She made a mental note to keep an eye out for an umbrella.

****

Ron switched to a camera overlooking the park and saw his men scouring it.

'Any sign of him yet?' he said into his radio. There was a pause and a crackle of static. The signal was very weak, and the voice kept breaking up.

'I can hardly hear you Sir. There's some terrible interference around today. We've been over the park a couple of times but there's no sign of him. I was about to call you'.

'OK. Forget the park. You can try the beach now. Our guest has moved away'.

He saw the guard fiddle with his radio, trying to improve the signal.

'Can.... go...the beach...y...Sir? W...finish...he...'

'Yes. Can you hear me? Go to the beach' Ron shouted into the radio emphasising the words. 'I repeat. Leave the park. Go to the beach'.

He saw the guard talking to his colleagues and the they all shrugged their shoulders. He said something else into his radio, but it was completely lost in the static and Ron couldn't understand a word of it.

'This is bloody hopeless' he muttered, tossing the radio aside. He turned to the guard that was monitoring Julie. 'Get out to the park as quick as you can and tell them to search the beach. This is turning into a sham. We're got to find out where that bastard is before he jeopardizes the whole operation'.

The guard scurried away and Ron returned to the screen, trying to find Zak.

'Where are you, you little prick. You can't hide from me all day'.

Chapter 15 – "Can I help You?"

When Zak left the pond, he had hurried towards the beach as he thought he could mingle in with the crowds. As he was approaching, he noticed how deserted it was and stopped dead in his tracks. This can't be right, he thought. If he had been in the middle of a thunderstorm in the winter, he might have understood the beach being empty, but on such a nice day as this it should have been packed.

He scanned the area and more by luck than judgement, he spotted a camera perched on top of one of the streetlamps. He ducked behind a wall and groaned, realising that he was still in the confines of the complex and still being monitored. He sat thinking while he watched the camera rotating from side to side. He couldn't hang around here. They'd be after him within minutes if they spotted him.

He waited for the camera to rotate away from him and darted along the road to a small shop. He burst through the door, relieved to find it unlocked, and slammed it shut behind him, dropping to the floor below the level of the glass panelled door. He lay on the floor breathing heavily with his back to the door.

'Can I help you?'

The voice made Zak jump and he sat up in shock, scanning the shop for the owner of the voice. He heard a scratching noise but couldn't see anyone. Then the voice came again.

'Good morning. Can I help you?'

He crawled across the floor to the counter and stuck his head around it, but there was no one there.

'Can I help you? Rarrr'.

The penny dropped. He was in a pet shop. At the far end of the room was a cage with a parrot running up and down its perch chattering away merrily.

'Can I help you? Good morning. Close the door. Rarrr'.

When Zak was away from the window, he stood up and wandered over to the parrot.

'Hello Polly', he said putting his fingers through the bars of the cage and stroking the bird's feathers. He noticed that the food bowl was empty. 'Are you hungry?'.

'Can I help you? Mind the step', said the bird.

Zak looked around. 'Hello?' he called. 'Anyone here?'. There was no reply.

He found some birdseed and filled the parrot's bowl who ate it hungrily. There were no other animals in the shop. Other than the parrot, he was alone. He had a quick scout around to see if he could find anything useful but didn't come up with much. It was a pet shop after all. He did find a back door though that backed onto an empty car park, and there weren't any cameras as far as he could see.

He returned to the shop and sank down to the floor to think. His escape from the underground complex had lifted his spirits, but now his mood darkened again. How big is this place? And where the hell am I? Nothing made much sense to him. He had just run away from the only person who could give him any answers and he didn't intend on going back.

After a few minutes pondering, he decided he wasn't going to gain anything by sitting still and waiting to be found. Keep moving, a voice inside said to him. Good advice, he thought getting up. If he could manage to evade the watchful eye of the cameras for a while, at least he'd be able to check out the place. He poured the remainder of the bird seed into the cage and left by the back door.

'Close the door. Can I help you? Have a nice day' squawked the parrot happily. Hmm – fat chance, thought Zak.

He dashed across the car park, keeping an eye out for any movement, human or otherwise. He headed away from the beach and followed a narrow path for about half a mile before spotting the next camera. Again, it was perched upon a streetlamp, tracking slowly back and forth as if it was watching a tennis match in slow motion.

Zak darted behind a tree that was situated conveniently nearby Unfortunately, there was nothing else around to shield him. He checked his pockets and found he was still carrying the length of rope and the strange gun. Everything else had vanished, probably washed away in the pond, he mused. The rope might come in handy, but it wasn't really going to give him much cover from the camera. He tried the gun, aiming it into the lens when it tracked his way. Nothing happened. Hardly surprising really, he thought. But then again, it had destroyed the strange bird and the rabbit. Anything was worth a try in this place. He put the gun and the rope back in his pocket and searched the ground around him. After a frantic search, he found a handful of fairly large stones. He stood up and waited for the camera to move out of his line of vision. Taking careful aim, he lobbed the first stone and was surprised at how close he was. The stone smashed into the lamppost just below his target and bounced back toward him. His confidence leapt at this close shot and he threw the rest of the stones in quick succession, only to realise that his first attempt had been somewhat lucky. He didn't even hit the lamppost again.

He ducked behind the tree again and searched for more stones. Only four. The next two shots went wide too, and he hesitated before throwing the third. Again, he missed, and he swore as the camera came back. One more chance, he thought, breathing heavily from the exertion of his efforts. No chance said his inner voice. You've missed ten times already. What chance have you got? He glanced around the tree again and was about to throw the stone when he had a better idea. He waited until the camera was turned completely away from him, and then sprinted for the lamppost. He arrived as the camera turned back and stood up straight against it so he wouldn't be seen. He retrieved the rope from his pocket and looped it around the lamppost and his body, tying it tightly behind his back. He didn't know why he hadn't thought of this before. He had done it on a number of occasions when breaking in to first floor windows. He leaned back against the rope and used it as a support as he climbed the post like a monkey, hand over hand, making sure he was behind the camera at all times. It was a bit higher than he was used to, but it didn't deter him. He reached the top after a couple of minutes and quickly grabbed the stone from his pocket where he had put it. He resisted the urge to pull a face into the camera and prepared to smash it with the stone. He raised it over his head…..and slipped.

    The rope managed to take most of his weight as he frantically grabbed at the post, but he smashed his face into it, scraping a long line of skin against the concrete pillar. Blinding pain flashed through the side of his face and he screamed in agony. Somehow, he managed to keep a grip on the post, but the stone slipped from his hand and tumbled to the ground, bouncing on the path below with a dull thud. He groaned, gripping at the post in frustration and puffing hard. A trickle of blood ran down his face and dropped off, following the stone. He hoisted himself up again and examined the camera. He couldn't smash it now, but he might be able to wedge something in it so that it couldn't turn. He mentally searched his pockets again but knew that he wasn't carrying anything.

    The strength was diminishing rapidly from his arms and he knew that he wouldn't make it down and up again without a long rest first. He pushed up with his feet to get a better grip and suddenly realised that he *was* carrying something. It wasn't the best idea he had all day, but he decided to give it a go. He reached down and carefully grabbed he trainer from his foot, nearly slipping again in the process. As the camera turned, he wedged the shoe into the gap it had made. The camera made an attempt to turn back but got stuck fast facing the way he had come. He heaved a sigh of relief and made a hasty retreat down the lamppost. He rested for a while at the bottom, pleased at his ingenuity, but not looking forward to travelling with one shoe.

He retrieved the rope from the lamppost and continued his journey down the path and had only gone a few steps when he discarded the other shoe and tossed it aside. There must be a shop with shoes somewhere he thought. The hot sun beat down and burned the pavement, and in turn, the pavement burned the soles of his feet.

Chapter 16 – "The fairground"

Julie left the beach, and to her relief the mysterious balloons stopped appearing. She was glad of the large brimmed sun hat that she had acquired. Initially it was to protect her from the balloon's water, but now it was doing a good job keeping the hot sun off her head. She walked in the opposite direction to the town centre, back towards the strange house where she had woken up. Humbug followed obediently panting, his tail giving an occasional wag of contentment. He was having a better day than she was.

As she walked, she tried to think of some kind of action plan. She'd been on the move most of the day and hadn't seen anyone. Except the poor young girl on the skates, an inner voice reminded her. She shuddered and quickly pushed the voice aside. She had come to the conclusion that for some reason unknown to her, she had been kidnapped by someone, also unknown to her, and was being held as a prisoner in a large complex, also completely unknown to her. She frowned. It's not looking good, she thought. If only her abductor would put in an appearance so that she might get a few answers, even if they weren't the answers she wanted. Anything was better than not knowing what was going on.

At the moment she figured that she had two choices. One was to keep walking, scan the area and see what she could learn of her whereabouts. The alternative was to return to the house and wait for someone to show up and give her some kind of an explanation. She had a strong urge to do just that, but she had no idea how long she would have to wait for. Might as well enjoy the weather while it lasts. It could be raining tomorrow.

Who said I'd still be here tomorrow? Think positive. Look on the bright side of this. She racked her brain but couldn't come up with a bright side.

She shrugged her shoulders with a sigh and bent down to pet the small dog. As she stood up, she thought she heard a sound. Did I imagine that? Sounds like music. No, there it is again.

The music was muffled, coming from quite a distance but could just be heard. Humbug pricked up his ears and gave a yap as he heard it too. As she headed towards the sound, she realised that it was a funfair, the music blaring out from various different rides and combining to produce a din in which no particular song could be heard clearly. A bit of the Beach Boys "Surfin' U.S.A.", a fragment of a Madonna song, all overshadowed by a loud thumping bass that could have been any number of dance records. There was something wrong about the sound though, and it didn't take Julie long to figure out that it was the lack of voices. All fairground music was normally drowned out by the hordes of shrieking teenagers enjoying their favourite rides.

But not here. The lack of atmosphere was apparent even before she entered the main gates containing a large sign:-

WELL'S TRAVELLING FAMILY FUNFAIR

KEEPING YOU ENTERTAINED SINCE 1895

There were no shuffling crowds, no excited screaming, nobody willing you to have one more go at trying to throw a hoop over a large jar of sweets with a ten-pound note stuck to it. As a "family funfair", it was the most un-family like place she had been to. What was surprising, however, was the fact that every ride seemed to be in operation as if it was a full house. All the lights were flashing, the rides stopping every three minutes, unloading invisible passengers, and taking on equally invisible unsuspecting victims. It all seemed like a strange dream. She could imagine waking up after her heavy night on the town and having dreamt the whole thing. If only it was, she thought miserably.

She walked slowly around the fairground in the hope that there might be somebody somewhere, but nobody showed up. After a few minutes, she had the uncanny feeling that she was being watched though. Perhaps it was the strange atmosphere that produced this feeling, but the more she thought about it the more it made sense.

The phone call in the town centre had occurred just as she was passing the phone box.

The balloons had followed her when she was at the beach.

If someone had kidnapped her and left her to roam around, it was logical that they would want to keep an eye on her. She hastily looked over her shoulder, a crazy image of a madman stalking her flashed through her mind. If the madman was there, he was as invisible as everyone else. She shivered. The realisation that she was probably being watched unnerved her again. She had just about got a grip after the incident with the floating balloons, but now the uneasy feeling returned.

She turned to leave but realised that Humbug had vanished. He had been there a second ago. She had become very attached to the little dog. He was the only company she had had since her nightmare day had begun. Before she could start looking for him, a flash of red appeared before her in the shape of a large balloon. She screamed and pulled her hat on tight, anticipating the drenching that was about to follow. The balloon hovered in front of her though and didn't rise above her head like the others had done. As she watched it, it rotated slowly around, and she noticed that there were words written on it. Her eyes widened in amazement when she read the message….

"Help me. Ghost Train. Jenny".

She screamed as the balloon burst with a loud bang.

****

Zak was in a lot of pain. The heat of the pavement seemed to intensify with every step that he took. A blister was beginning to form on the sole of his left foot, and he knew it wouldn't be long before the other one would follow in sympathy. He sat down on the hot pavement for a rest and examined his aching feet. He realised that he wouldn't be able to go much further like this, so he tore his shirt into two pieces and carefully bandaged them. It wouldn't be very comfortable, but it would help with the pain he was experiencing. After a few minutes he gingerly got to his feet and tested his makeshift shoes. It wasn't perfect but it was a lot better. He hobbled on, keeping one eye out for cameras and another for a shop where he might be able to improve his footwear. A third eye would have come in handy as he turned a corner and almost ran straight into Martin Briggs.

Briggs was the unfortunate guard who had been sent to inform his unit in the park to move on to the beach. He had hurried from the underground complex through the hole in the pond as it was the most direct way. If he had gone through the proper exit, which was hidden further up the beach, he would never have run into Zak.

The both jumped in shocked, but Zak recovered quicker and, realising it was a guard, did the first thing that came into his head. He kicked out, karate style and sent Briggs flying backward clutching his stomach and gasping where he'd been winded. Zak would regret this move later as the force of the blow finally burst the blister on his foot and the pain caused him to fall backwards too, screaming. Again, he recovered first, just in time to see the security guard fumble for his radio. He threw himself at him and wrenched the radio from his hand, putting a knee into Briggs' podgy stomach. Briggs collapsed again trying to draw fresh air into his lungs but having great difficulty. Zak turned him over and bent an arm up behind his back as far as he could. The guard tried to scream but all that came out was a rush of silent wind.

'OK. I want some answers' said Zak. 'What the hell's going on here? Are you Ron?'

The guard didn't answer so Zak put some pressure on the arm. It seemed to help.

'Argggh. No. Ron sent me. To fetch the others. They're looking for you' said Briggs in-between screaming and trying to catch his breath. 'In the park'.

'Where is he? Where's Ron?'. More pressure.

'He's……He's inside. In the complex'.

'Whereabouts in the complex?'

'The control room, the control room'. Briggs voice rose in pitch as his arm was bent even further behind his back. The pain was almost unbearable. Zak had a million questions he wanted to ask. He didn't know where to start.

'Why am I here? What does Ron want me for?'

'Argggh. I don't know. I swear I don't know'. Briggs was losing his vision and the world was beginning to swim away.

'Tell me' screamed Zak, giving an extra hard push on the arm.

Unfortunately, It was just a bit too much and Briggs collapsed into unconsciousness.

'Shit'. Zak dropped the limp body and sighed in dismay. He grabbed the radio and switched it on. He could hear a crackle of static, but nobody was broadcasting at the moment. He left it switched on, turning the volume to low, and clipped it to his belt. He quickly searched the guard and found a small wallet with an ID card and what looked like a pass card into the complex. He read the name on the ID.

'Well Briggs, looks like you could be in deep shit when your boss finds you'.

He removed the shirt that was wrapped around his feet and pulled off Brigg's shoes. A bit big, but a lot better than a rolled-up shirt. He considered swapping clothes with the guard but realised that the size difference would be too great. Briggs was a good eight inches shorter than him; his height being compensated by a much larger than average stomach. Zak retrieved the rope from his pocket and dragged the man's body to the trees at the side of the path. He quickly tied him to one, making sure he couldn't be seen if anyone was to pass by. The remains of his shirt made quite a useful gag, although a bit on the putrid side. Still, he probably won't come around for a while, thought Zak with a smile.

He jumped to his feet and looked both ways up the path. He didn't want to run straight into the rest of this merry bunch. He had managed to handle this one but didn't fancy his chances if he was outnumbered. He didn't want to go back to the complex either, even with the pass card. He saw a turning further up the path running East-West to the one he was currently on. He shrugged and headed for it.

At the intersection was a signpost. One way was a fairground, the other a church. I've had enough games for one day, thought Zak. He turned towards the church and limped on, the blister on his foot giving him a painful greeting once again. Despite the pain, he was beginning to feel more confident after his victory over Briggs. Perhaps I'll find a way out yet, he thought.

****

The church seemed somewhat out of place in the complex. It was a large, old fashioned church with crumbling walls and cracked windows. It looked as if it hadn't been used in a long time, and the churchyard had become overrun with weeds and long tangled grass.

He explored the neglected church and after finding nothing of interest, he climbed the steep, rickety steps to the bell tower which commanded the greatest view of the surrounding area. There seems to be no outer limit to this "prison" he marvelled, staring out over the small town before him. He could see the beach from here and could just make out some windows to a small cottage with the pond that he'd escaped from. No – not a cottage, more like a giant shed. As he gazed out, he realised for the first time in a while that he was hungry. He hadn't eaten since breakfast. Even prisoners get hungry occasionally, he thought looking at his watch. 4:45. Where had the day gone? He wished he'd headed towards the funfair now. He might have found a bite to eat there. He considered doubling back and looking for a shop but decided it was best to stay put and lie low for a while. It wouldn't be long before Briggs was discovered. He didn't want to risk running into anyone and being dragged back inside.

He walked the church again. Surely there must be something to eat somewhere here. A drink wouldn't go amiss either. He stopped suddenly as he saw some steps leading down at the side of the main church hall. He hurried towards them and realised they led to a cellar. The steps were steep and narrow, and Zak nearly fell a couple of times. He walked along a dim passageway, the only light coming from above, helping him find his way. The passage began to open out and Zak found himself in a small room that was lit by a number of candles.

Candles? How can there be candles here? Someone must have lit them recently. It was then that he noticed a mattress had been set out in the corner, with blankets tossed over it, and he gasped as he realised that someone must be living here.

He heard a noise behind him and spun round frantically, his heart suddenly finding that familiar pounding that he had experienced many times in the last couple of days. A bright light was shining in his face and he was temporarily blinded, unable to see who was there.

'Put your hands over your head. Don't try anything stupid'. The voice was accompanied by a sharp pain as the unforeseen figure poked, what felt like a spear, into his stomach.

'OK. OK. Don't do anything rash' said Zak, obliging. Whoever it was must be a prisoner too. Why else would they be holing themselves up in here? The light dropped from his eyes and Zak blinked a few times in quick succession to get his vision back. A figure was standing before him holding a long sharp stick out as a weapon. As his eyesight returned to normal, he got a proper look at his adversary. Standing before him was a fourteen-year-old boy.

Chapter 17 – "Randy"

Julie stared in astonishment at the remains of the balloon, questions popping in and out of her mind at lightning speed. Jenny? Could Jenny be involved in this too? Is she here somewhere? Or is this a hoax just to catch me? She turned towards the ghost train, stopped, started again, took a few paces and hesitated.

'This is crazy' she said aloud. 'How the hell can Jenny be here? How would she have got a message to me on a balloon? It must be a trick'.

But what if it wasn't? What if her friend was in trouble and needed her? What if she ignored the message and something happened to Jenny? Something gruesome. Just like the girl on the roller skates.

She headed towards the ghost train again, bolder than before, but again stopped short, wishing she knew what to do. She finally decided to go in. What have I got to lose, she reasoned? If they want to catch me, I can't really stop them. They could just walk up to me and lead me away. There's nobody to call for help.

This last thought was somewhat alarming, and she nearly changed her mind. She started tentatively towards the ghost train again, watching it loom up over her as she got closer, feeling like it was beckoning her, daring her to step inside to see the horrors within.

As she approached it, she remembered that Humbug had vanished. She would feel better if he was with her, but the little dog was nowhere to be seen. A car crashed through the swing doors at the far end of the track making her jump, and it slowed to a stop in front of her. She took a deep breath, considered changing her mind again, and then stepped into the car and sat down before she had a chance to do so. Her heart started to hammer in her chest as she heard the mechanism start up and the car lurched forward. The door in front of her depicted a huge clown's face with a menacing grin and blue hypnotic eyes. The eyes were the last thing she saw as the doors were flung open and the ghost train swallowed the small car that she sat in. The sounds of laughter filled her ears as the doors swung shut plunging her into blackness.

****

Ron watched as Julie disappeared into the ghost train and flicked a switch on his panel so he could see her re-appear inside. He had decided that while Zak was on the loose, he had better keep Julie out of the way. He wasn't ready for them to meet yet. He wanted to ensure that everything was organised before introducing them to each other. As long as Zak was on the run, things were a mess. Actually, things are completely fucked up, he thought angrily. He had completely under-estimated Zak. He had not only managed to escape but also to stay hidden, despite the immense surveillance system that was installed in the complex. Even with a unit of guards scouring the area, he hadn't been found yet.

He watched Julie's car move slowly along the track and flicked a switch causing her car to slow to a halt. Another switch automatically locked the large doors on either end of the ride. He watched her frantically look from one side to the other as the bolts clicked shut and then switched the monitor to another camera. Julie would be safe for a while. Zak was another matter entirely. He had to be found.

****

The boy held his makeshift spear firmly against Zak's chest as he spoke 'Who are you? What are you doing here?'

'You're just a kid', said Zak in amazement. 'Why are they holding you? What do they want you for?'

'I'm asking the questions' said the boy pushing the stick deeper into Zak's chest and drawing a spot of blood. 'Answer me. What's your name?'

Zak wasn't afraid of the boy, but while he was holding the stick with the lethally sharpened tip, he thought best not to agitate him.

'My name is Zak' he said, taking a step back and wiping the blood away with the palm of his hand. 'As far as I can tell, I have been kidnapped by a man called Ron, but I don't know why. I escaped from an underground complex earlier today and I've been running around since, looking for a way out of this place, and trying not to get caught'. He laughed at the irony of being "caught" by this small boy, and then suddenly grabbed the stick and twisted it out of his hands.

'You're the first person I've seen, other than an unfortunate associate of Ron's'. He smiled as the boy's eyes widened in horror at losing his weapon. 'You wouldn't stand a chance if you were caught you know'.

The boy turned and ran, but Zak was after him instantly. He grabbed the boy by the back of his shirt and dragged him back towards the candlelit room.

'Let me go. I didn't mean to hurt you' cried the boy. Zak pushed him to the floor and stood so that he blocked the way out.

'Right. My turn to ask some questions. We might as well be civilised about this. What's your name?'

'Randy' said the boy sulkily 'Can I have my spear back?'.

Zak ignored the question. 'How did you get here? I mean, how did you get into the complex?'

'I live here. With my sister'.

'What do you mean, you live here?'

'Like I said. I live here. That's my bed'. He indicated the mattress. 'Ruby – That's my sister, sleeps next door'.

'But how did you get here? Where are your parents?'

'My mum's dead' said the boy distantly. 'I'm looking after Ruby now. Please give me my spear back'.

'How did your mum die? What about your dad?' Zak was shocked. He couldn't believe that this young boy was actually living here. What could Ron possibly want him for.

'I don't know where my dad is. They said he disappeared when mum died. Can I go now? I want to find my sister'.

'Where is your sister? Ruby?'

'Don't know. She went out skating. She likes to skate. She should be back by now. I've got to find her. They might have caught her'.

'How old is she?'

'Ruby's ten. Can I go look for her now?'

'Can I come with you? I want to talk some more'.

'If you want' whined the boy. He didn't seem too keen on the idea.

'Here. You might need this' said Zak, tossing him the stick. 'If you try to use it on me again, I'll break it in half' he warned.

The boy grabbed the stick and darted past Zak and up the steps. Zak dashed after him but tripped on the bottom step, bashing his knee painfully. Randy didn't look back and disappeared through the entrance into the church hall, not slowing down. Zak jumped up ignoring the pain flaring through his leg and chased after the boy. He saw him running out of the main entrance of the church and continuing across the churchyard to a dirt track that ran all the way to the beach. He followed as fast as his blistered feet would allow, but the boy had a good head start and was running surprisingly fast for a fourteen-year old. As he got closer, he turned into a wooded area that ran alongside the track. Zak was gaining. He could hear the boy panting now and he was definitely slowing. Zak finally caught him as he burst out of the woods and back onto a path that looked vaguely familiar. The boy turned, wielding the pointed stick but didn't have the energy to be any great threat to Zak. Zak grabbed it and snapped it in two as promised. Randy collapsed, out of breath - a painful look on his face as he saw his treasured weapon destroyed.

Zak sat beside him and examined his knee. There was a large bruise already beginning to form and the skin was grazed badly. Could have been a lot worse, he thought. Randy was looking at the leg too.

'I didn't mean to hurt you. I just wanted to find my sister'. He began to cry.

'Don't worry. It's all right. Stop crying now. I'm not going to hurt you'. Zak wasn't used to children and he couldn't handle this.

Randy blinked a couple of times to clear his eyes and wiped his sleeve across his runny nose. He seemed to make a quick recovery and Zak wondered how much of it was an act.

'OK. Are you feeling better now?'

The boy nodded and sniffed. 'You didn't have to break my spear'.

Zak smiled. 'Let's go and find your sister. Which way?'

Randy pointed up the path and Zak followed the finger, instantly recognising the path that he had been on earlier. Actually, it all looked a bit *too* familiar. He turned around and his whole body sagged in despair. He was sitting just up the road from the lamppost with the camera mounted on it. He could still see his shoe holding the camera firmly in place so that the lens was directed straight at him. He could almost feel Ron's eyes gazing at him through the lens, watching.

Zak jumped up and grabbed the boy as he heard Ron's orders being barked through the radio that was still attached to his belt.

'He's in sector nine. I repeat, sector nine. All units surround the area immediately'.

Zak scanned both directions wishing he knew which way they would be coming from. The boy grabbed his sleeve.

'Follow me. I know where to go'.

Zak obliged. The boy obviously knew the area better than him. As they ran, Zak turned towards the camera and couldn't resist waving.

Chapter 18 – "The tunnel"

Julie knew that she had been tricked as soon as her car had stopped, but she called out anyway.

'Jenny. Are you there? Are you alright?'

When there was no response, she kicked herself for being led so easily. She got out of the car and felt her way along the wall to the entrance she had just come through. There was a little bit of light seeping under the doors which helped but there was no internal light at all. She reached the door and pushed. Locked, as she suspected. She tried giving the door a good kick, but it was more solid than it looked, and it hardly moved.

'OK. Why am I here?' she asked out loud. 'Why do you want me here? Can you at least tell me that?' Her voice began to crack. The toils of the day were finally catching up on her and she was tired and scared. She slumped down by the door and began to cry. The worst thing was not knowing anything. It was so frustrating being kidnapped and held prisoner but know knowing why she was being held or who was holding her.

She sat for ten minutes, realising that nobody was there to greet her. The long day and heavy evening the night before finally caught up with her and she closed her eyes and fell into a fitful sleep. She dreamt of funfairs and telephones and strange balloons that went bang in the night.

****

'Where are we going?' asked Zak as they hurried back through the woods.

'I know a secret passage. I use it to stay hidden from them'.

'What do you know about them?'

The boy ignored him as they dashed back up the dirt track. Zak followed. He could ask questions later when they were safe. If they were safe, he corrected himself.

Randy ran through the churchyard and around the side of the church to some steps leading down toward a small door. He pulled the door open and the smell of grease and petrol wafted through. It was strong. Randy ignored it and Zak followed him into the room, gagging at the taste of the air as it caught in his throat.

'Help me move this' said the boy puffing and grabbing at a large workbench.

Zak grabbed it and dragged it to the side of the room, spilling a can of oil out of the door as he did so. In the brief few seconds that he had been in there he'd established that it was some kind of gardener's storeroom. There was a large petrol lawnmower in the corner and various other devices for keeping the church gardens in order. He spotted a chainsaw and grabbed at it as Randy scrabbled about on the floor. He had his fingers wrapped around a ring of a trapdoor that was hidden under the workbench and was struggling to pull it up. Zak took over and the boy darted to a shelf and grabbed a couple of long handled torches he had taken from a shop on his last trip to town. He stuffed his pockets with batteries too and then closed the door to the shed, plunging them into darkness. The torch light flicked on a second later and strange shadows danced around the room. He thrust the torch into Zak's hand and switched the other one on as he jumped down the hole. Zak took another quick scan of the room before throwing the chainsaw over his shoulder and following.

'Pull the door shut'.

The boy seemed quite a way ahead of him already and his voice echoed around the tunnel making it bounce around and hit Zak from all directions. He pulled the trapdoor down with a large crash that took a few seconds to disperse. He was standing on a platform that was five feet below the floor of the storeroom and had to stoop as he walked along. The tunnel started to go down, and after a while he found he could stand upright again.

'What is this place?' he said. 'How did you find it?'

'I was snooping around and just came across it' replied Randy with a grin. 'Pretty neat isn't it?'

'Pretty neat' whispered Zak under his breath.

The walls of the tunnel were solid rock. It looked as if was old. Not just a few years old, but hundreds of years old. There was a damp, rotten smell about the whole place probably coming from the floor of the tunnel which was the wettest part. There were puddles here and there where the rain had soaked through from above. The roof of the tunnel was made of rock too and had cracked and broken in many places.

'Is it safe in here? Have you been this far in before?' asked Zak, prodding at the rock above his head and jumping as a large chunk crumbled away.

'I've been all the way through' said the boy proudly. 'It's not too bad here. It gets worse the closer you get'.

'The closer you get to where? Where does it lead to?'

'The beach. It comes out in a cave in the bay. Can't you tell? We're going downwards all the time'.

'The beach?' said Zak astounded. 'It must be over a mile long'.

'Probably' said the boy with a shrug. 'I bet it was used by smugglers once. That's what I think it is. A smugglers tunnel'.

Zak thought he might be right. He couldn't see why it came up in the church though. It seemed a very unlikely place for smugglers. He didn't voice his opinion though. He had other things he wanted to talk about.

'You said that you've used this tunnel to stay hidden from them' said Zak jumping over a puddle and nearly losing his balance. He steadied himself and continued after the nimble footed boy. 'What do you know about them? Who are they?'

'I don't know them' said the boy. 'They said they would look after us when my mum died. I don't like them though. They're not nice to me like my mum was. That's why we live out here. We ran away'.

'When did you run away? How long have you been sleeping in the church?'

'About a week. They haven't found us yet. We hide down here if we see anyone'.

Zak couldn't believe that they had been lucky enough to stay hidden for a week, especially if Ruby went off skating. He had found Randy in less than a day. Ron must be far more concerned about me he thought.

'When did your mum die?' he asked gently, not wanting to upset the boy. 'I mean. How long have you been here overall?'

'Mum died a couple of years ago' said Randy. 'When they first brought us here, they were nice to us. They used to take us to the funfair and the beach'.

'Didn't you think it was strange that there was nobody else here? No other children around'.

'They told us that the funfair was just for us. That they got it especially for us. I believed them at first. I think I was too young to understand that something was wrong. But I know now. That's why I ran away. I was hoping to find someone else'. He stopped and turned to face Zak for the first time since they had been speaking. 'How did you get here? You said you were kidnapped. How did it happen?'

'I wish I knew' said Zak, stopping and resting his knee which was now beginning to go stiff 'I just woke up here. The last thing I remember was walking into a prison cell'.

'You were a prisoner?' gasped Randy in amazement. 'How could they kidnap you from a prison?'

'That's a good question' said Zak. 'I've not really thought about it. The people guarding the prison must have something to do with this'.

'Why were you in prison?'

'I wasn't actually convicted' said Zak. 'I was wrongly accused of killing someone. They were about to lock me up and throw away the key. If I ever get out of here, I'm going to be a prisoner all over again'.

This was the first time he'd actually thought of this and it didn't help his state of mind much. What's the point in trying to escape, only to be locked up again? He might as well just walk out and see what Ron wanted him for.

'Couldn't you hide?' asked Randy. 'I mean. If you get out of here. I could help you. I'm good at hiding.

Zak smiled. 'Let's see If we can get out of here first', he said. 'It might be a bit harder than you think'.

****

Suddenly the radio burst into life making Zak and Randy jump.

'We've lost them Sir. We surrounded the church and moved in but there's no sign of them. They've just disappeared'.

'How could they disappear? Check the area again. They're in there somewhere'. Ron was getting frantic and swore under his breath. 'Make sure you search every possible hiding place in that church – but keep the outskirts covered. I don't want them to slip past you and find Julie'.

'Who's Julie?' asked Zak. 'Does he call your sister Julie?'

Randy shook his head.

'Did you ever see anyone else in the complex? Was there anyone other than you and Ruby?'

'No'. Randy shrugged his shoulders. 'If there was, they were kept well hidden'.

Zak turned his attention back to the radio, but the voices had stopped broadcasting. He turned the radio up so that he wouldn't miss anything and started down the tunnel again.

'It looks as if we're not the only ones here' he said as the boy scurried after him. 'If Ron has kidnapped someone else then I want to find her. She might have a better idea of what's going on'.

'But she could be anywhere. This place is pretty big you know'. Randy stumbled and fell into Zak, nearly causing him to lose his balance. They steadied themselves and moved on.

'I'm hoping that Ron will let something slip before he discovers I've got Briggs' radio. How much further is it? We must be near the sea by now'. The water level was beginning to rise and was now lapping over Zak's ankles.

'It's quite a way yet. If the tides in, the water will be up to your knees by the time we get out'.

A couple of minutes later Randy stopped. 'Couldn't we use the radio? Pretend to be one of them. We could tell Ron that we've been spotted somewhere else. It would keep them away from us'.

'It might work' said Zak doubtfully. 'I wonder if they can trace the location if he recognises my voice'.

'It's worth a try isn't it?'

'We'll wait until we get out of the tunnel. I don't want to have a party waiting for us at the other end'.

As Zak spoke, an excited voice came over the radio. 'Sir. I think I know where they are. There's a trapdoor at the back of the church with some freshly spilt oil nearby. They must have gone inside'.

'Shit. That tunnel leads right through to the beach' said Ron. 'Get some men down there now. If we're quick, we'll have them cornered'. He cursed. He had forgotten the tunnel was there. It had been years since he'd used it.

'We're on our way Sir'.

****

Zak and Randy looked at each other in despair and started running down the tunnel as quick as the flowing water would allow.

'How long will it take them to reach the beach?' said Zak as he leapt over a low wall of rock.

'Less than ten minutes' replied Randy. 'If they're quick' he added breathlessly.

'And what about us? Are we going to make it?

'We should do. It's a lot slower to move down here. It will be close. There might be a problem though'.

'What's that?'. Zak could do without problems at the moment.

'There's nowhere to go when we get out. It's a cliff face, leading to an open beach. It will take us a good few minutes to find a place to hide'.

Zak groaned and nearly stopped to consider options but managed to keep going. He would worry about that when he got there. Let's just focus on one thing at a time, he thought.

The water level was getting higher and Zak was about to ask Randy how far it was again when he saw a light in the distance. 'We're nearly there. Just a bit further. Are you OK?'.

The boy was struggling to catch his breath. The log awkward run was affecting him much more than Zak.

'I'm.....OK.....Don't…..worry….keep…..moving'.

The light got closer and soon the tunnel widened into a dank, seaweed smelling cave. Zak ran to the entrance of the tunnel, turning his torch off and carefully peeked out. Nobody around yet. At least they had won the race, but they still had to hide somewhere. The water was over his knees now and the wall of rock ran a good sixty yards in each direction as Randy had suggested. They had a lot of water to get through before they could even get off the beach. Randy caught up and nearly ran into him.

'Did we beat them? Have you found somewhere to hide?'

'Yes, and No. In that order'. Zak was thinking fast. He waded out and looked both ways up the sea front. Still no sign of them but no obvious hiding place either.

He had an idea.

'Follow me. Bring your torch and keep your head low'. He waded out further, unscrewing both ends of his torch as he did so. He still had the chainsaw around his neck which made things difficult, but he was reluctant to let his only weapon go. Not that the saltwater would do it any good, he mused. He passed the radio to Randy and knelt down so that just his head was above the water and pulled the torch apart, emptying the batteries into the sea. He pulled the bulb and glass out of the front which left him with the long thin casing which was hollow all the way through.

'Do the same with yours' he said. 'Quickly. They'll be here any minute'.

He glanced up and noticed that they were still alone. 'Just a sec. Give me that back. It's worth a try while it's still dry'. He took the radio back from Randy and pushed the button.

'Sir. It's Briggs Sir. I can't find anyone in the park. Did they move out?'. He managed to disguise his voice, but he didn't think it sounded anything like Briggs.

'Briggs? Get down to the sea front at once'. Ron was obviously too stressed to realise the difference'. 'We think we might have got him. And the kid too'.

'Yes Sir. On my way. By the way, I thought I saw Julie a moment ago. Isn't anyone watching her?'

'You can't have' said Ron checking the monitor and seeing Julie fast asleep in the ghost train. She's still up at the fair. Sleeping like a baby'.

Zak smiled. Found her.

'Sorry Sir. Must be my eyes playing tricks on me. I'm on my way'. He clipped the radio back to his belt and nervously glanced up again. The first guard came into view, heading down the hill towards the beach.

He quickly shoved one end of the torch tube into his mouth – it wasn't much bigger than the size of the battery and it fit quite comfortably. Randy copied him, realising what he was doing and they both ducked under, leaving a couple of inches of their tubes above the surface of the water. As a snorkel it was by no means perfect, but it seemed to work. He grabbed the boy's hand and led him along, trying to keep parallel to the beach, using the depth of the water as a rough guide.

From a distance, the two small tubes sticking up looked like leaves floating in the murky water.

Chapter 19 – "The Ghost Train"

Zak popped his head out of the water and was amazed to see how far they had gone. He hoped they would be out of sight, but they had actually travelled about half a mile. He pulled Randy out of the water and they swam ashore, rubbing their eyes to get the salty water out of them. He still had the chainsaw slung over his shoulder and he dumped it next to him as he collapsed by the beach wall. It might still work if it dried out, but he was doubtful. They had been underwater for quite a while. He put the two plastic tubes in a pocket, hoping they wouldn't be needed again.

'You OK?' he said to the boy.

'My eyes are stinging' said Randy rubbing them with both hands. 'Other than that, I'm fine. Good plan'.

Zak laughed. 'It wasn't bad considering the circumstances'. He felt better than he had in a long time. Not only had they managed to escape from the tunnel, but he now knew where Julie was hidden – whoever Julie was.

'Do you know the way to the fairground?' he asked.

'Yes. Do you think Ruby might be there?' replied Randy hopefully. Zak had forgotten all about Ruby. He hoped she was alright.

'She might be' he said. 'Let's go and see. We might find Ruby and Julie together. Keep your eye out for cameras though. I don't want to be spotted'.

'I know most of the cameras' said Randy, 'but it might be worth waiting until it gets dark? It would be harder for them to spot us when the sun's gone'.

Zak checked his watch. It was still going despite the soaking it had had. Six-twenty.

'Let's keep moving. It'll be a couple of hours before it even starts to get dark, and Ron's probably got infrared cameras anyway. With any luck they'll still be checking the tunnel. We should be safe for a while'.

The boy nodded in agreement and they set off. Zak wondered if it was worth bringing the chainsaw, but reluctantly decided to leave it on the beach. He wasn't sure whether he would be able to use it as a weapon anyway. The thought of slicing into someone with its sharp teeth made him shiver. He could always come back for it later if necessary.

'There's a beach shop up here' said Randy as they walked along the street, glancing around for cameras or any movement. 'We could get some dry clothes. There might be towels as well'.

'Good idea. I could do with some food too. I haven't eaten all day'.

The found some beach towels in the shop and dried themselves thoroughly. The only clothes they could find were shorts and tee shirts, but they were better than the wet clothes they were in.

'It's going to get cold later' said Zak. 'We'll have to try and find something warmer. There's no food though' he said glumly.

'There's plenty of other shops further up' said Randy brightly. 'We should find something'.

Zak bundled up the wet clothes and grabbed a bag to put them in. As he did this, the strange gun fell from his pocket. Randy picked it up.

'Wow. A gun. Where did you get this?'

Zak told him about the mechanical toys that Ron had in the complex. 'The gun seems to destroy them. It only shoots light as far as I can tell though. I did wonder why Ron bothered giving it to me, but I think he was just trying to amuse himself'.

'It's not bugged is it?' asked the boy wide-eyed.

'It can't be. If it was then we'd be under lock and key by now. It just shoots light. Pretty silly really'. He pulled the trigger to show the boy what he meant, and a thin beam of light fell on the far wall. He stuffed it in the bag with the clothes and they left the shop.

They found a newsagent further up and helped themselves to crisps and chocolate.

'Who keeps the shops stocked up with the food?' asked Zak. 'And why bother? It's not as if there's many people using them'.

'Who cares' said Randy tucking greedily into the chocolate. 'As long as it tastes alright, I don't care who put it here'.

Zak laughed and opened his crisps, but it still puzzled him. Perhaps there weren't many food shops around to keep stocked up. Maybe the guards liked to have snacks as they wandered around.

A crackle of static from the radio broke his thoughts and he grabbed it in astonishment. It couldn't still be working could it?

'What's going on. Have you got them yet?'

'No Sir. We've sent a group of men in each side of the tunnel. They'll be bringing them out soon. Don't worry'.

Zak chuckled. 'I'm sure he'll start worrying when he finds that we're not in there' he said. 'Come on. Let's go to the fairground before he starts an all-out search party'.

They reached the fair without incident and Zak was surprised – as Julie was earlier – that it was all in operation.

'Is it always running like this? he asked, looking around the rides and stalls in amazement.

'No. They must have started it all up for Julie. Perhaps they wanted to lure her here.

'If that's right then we're walking right into the lion's den' said Zak glancing nervously around. I wonder where she is. This place is pretty big. She could be anywhere'.

'We could try calling her. Most of the guards will be down at the beach. We haven't bumped into anyone yet. Chances are they've locked her up somewhere'.

Zak considered this for a moment and then shook his head. 'No. Ron said that she was sleeping. They probably drugged her. I don't like the idea of shouting out. There could be microphones as well as cameras. Let's just have a scout around. See what we can find'.

They skirted the edge of the funfair, being careful to avoid the few cameras that they did see.

'If they do spot us, we'll know about it straight away', said Zak indicating the radio that was clipped to his brightly coloured shorts. 'We won't have long after that. They'll be on top of us in a matter of minutes'.

After ten minutes of fruitless searching, they found themselves beneath the big wheel as it slowed and finally stopped to relieve itself of its non-existent passengers. Randy had an idea.

'Let's ride the big wheel' he said. 'We'll be able to see the whole of the fairground from the top. It might help us to spot Julie. Or Ruby' he added.

'Could be a bit risky' said Zak. 'If anyone spots us, we'd be stuck. You go. I'll keep lookout'.

Randy dashed to the wheel and climbed in the seat that was waiting at the bottom. It was his favourite ride in the fair, made even more enjoyable by the fact that he had a job to do. As it started up, he waved to Zak as he became smaller. Once at the top of the ride he looked towards the sea. He could just about make out Ron's men gathered like ants, looking helplessly for Zak and himself. He grinned. It was like looking through a one-way mirror. They would never be able to spot him at the top of the wheel from where they were.

He concentrated on the fairground below looking for any movement, other than that of the many rides that continued relentlessly and pointlessly carrying their ghost-riders. It was the movement of everything else that made him spot the stillness of the ghost train. He watched it for three revolutions of the wheel, but nothing moved. The doors were shut and hadn't opened once to spew out cars in all the time he'd watched it. Seems like a logical place to hide, thought Randy as the ride slowed down. He checked the beach again, but nothing had changed. They still had time on their hands.

'She could be on the ghost train' he said after climbing out and walking over to where Zak was hidden, glancing nervously around. 'It's the only ride that's not running. She could be locked inside'.

'Well spotted' said Zak admiringly. This kid was resourceful. 'Let's go see'.

****

Julie woke suddenly with a stifled scream when she saw the darkness.

Where am I?

Inside the ghost train, she answered herself. What was that noise?

She'd been woken by a sudden banging noise right by her head. She realised a second later that someone was pushing at the door that she was sleeping by. She heard voices.

'Locked. Try the other one. I bet she's in there'. That was a kids' voice, she realised startled. I'm not being held hostage by a kid am I? They must be here to help me. She sat motionless all the same. She wanted to be sure.

'Hello. Is anyone in there? Julie?'. A man's voice.

Julie's heart skipped a beat when she heard her name. They didn't sound threatening, and she didn't want to stay locked in here any longer. What did she have to lose?

'Who's there?' she said.

'She's in there' said Zak to the boy. 'Hello, Are you Julie? Are you OK?'

'I'm locked in. Who are you?'

'My name's Zak. Hang on. We'll try and get you out of there. Don't worry'.

Zak realised that he wasn't going to be able to open the door by ramming it. It was too solid for that. 'I'm going to have to go back and get the chainsaw' he said to Randy. 'Do you want to stay and keep Julie company?'

'I'll get the chainsaw' said Randy, not liking the idea of making conversation with the girl. 'You can stay here. I know the roads better than you'.

Zak agreed. He wanted to find out more about Julie anyway, so he was glad when the boy volunteered.

'Be careful. You should be alright. The guards will still be at the beach. And careful you don't accidentally start the chainsaw and lop your arm off'.

Randy grinned. 'No problem. I'll be back before you know it'. He dashed off. Zak wasn't too worried. Randy had managed to avoid Ron and his men for nearly a week. A quick trip to the beach and back should present too much of a problem.

'You still there Julie?'

'Well I'm not going anywhere' she said sarcastically. 'What's going on? Where did you come from?'

Zak settled down on the floor of the ghost train and began his story.

'It started last Saturday. I was robbing a video store...'

****

Randy appeared at the entrance of the fairground as Zak was finishing his story.

'Do you have any idea what all of this is about' said Julie. 'Why does this Ron want us here?'

'I wish I knew' replied Zak. 'I do know that he didn't want me to find you. He's got an army of men looking for me at the moment. I don't know how much longer we can avoid them'.

Randy appeared beside him and collapsed, puffing. He dropped the chainsaw at Zak's feet. 'That thing's bloody heavy' he said. I wish I'd let you go now. It's too hot for all this hard work. I hope it still works after all that'.

Zak laughed and grabbed the saw.

'Stand back Julie. If this thing works OK, I'll have you out of there in seconds.

He grabbed the string on the chainsaw and pulled. The chainsaw spluttered and water gushed out. He tried again. It caught, but then died immediately.

'Come on' he muttered, pulling again. It took two more pulls before it roared to life. The noise was horrendous. If this doesn't bring Ron's men running, then nothing will, he thought. He swiftly turned to the door of the ghost train and attacked. The sharp teeth of the saw made light work of the clown's face. He carefully cut a hole, just big enough for Julie to get out. He didn't want to waste any time due to the amount of noise he was making. Less than a minute later, a square piece of wood dropped to the ground and Zak retreated, turning the saw off. Julie peered out of the hole squinting as the bright sunlight pierced her eyes. Two smiling faces peered back.

'Why are you wearing a sunhat?' asked Zak puzzled.

Chapter 20 – "Lights Out"

'All units to the fairground. I repeat. All units to the fairground'.

It was the last thing that Zak had wanted to hear but he had half expected it. He turned to the boy. 'Do you know any more good hideouts?' he asked hopefully. The boy shook his head. 'We've got to get out of here. Are you ready Julie?'

'Yes' she said, a little startled. She had suddenly become involved in a manhunt. It had taken her all afternoon to meet someone and suddenly she had an army after her.

They ran out of the fairground and headed along a path running parallel to the beach.

'I've got an idea' said Zak. 'Let's go back to the underground complex. I've got a key now. We can just stroll in. They'll probably spend all night searching outside for us. It will give us a bit of time to think'.

Julie wasn't over-enthusiastic about this idea, but she couldn't think of anything better.

'We'll go back in the same way I got out' said Zak, warming to the idea. 'Through the pond'. His mind was racing. If they could get into the complex, they might be able to find the control room and take Ron by surprise. They might even find a way out.

Randy led them away from the main path and down a narrow street. His knowledge of the small town was amazing. Zak now understood how he'd managed to avoid being captured all week. These backstreets weren't monitored by cameras and he'd bet that the guards didn't know that half of them even existed. It would be easy to get lost in here, he thought.

They joined the woodland, near where Randy and Zak had been seen earlier and Randy slowed under the cover of some thick trees.

'Can we have a rest?' he cried breathlessly. He hadn't quite recovered from his previous run to fetch the chainsaw. 'We'll be OK here for a while. We could even camp out for the night. They won't find us in a hurry'.

'No. Let's try and get inside' said Zak sitting down on a tree stump beside the boy. 'We're not going to get a better chance to escape than tonight. With so many people outside looking for us, there will be minimum security'.

'But it's still got cameras' argued Randy. 'We can't hide from them'.

Zak thought for a moment. 'They won't be looking inside the complex' he said adamantly. 'All the monitors will be trained on the outside cameras. We should be able to walk straight in without being seen. It's the last thing Ron will expect'.

Randy frowned. It was bold, but he wasn't convinced.

'Look' said Zak. 'If we stay outside, we just wait until we get caught. We can't do anything else out here. If we go inside, we might just get lucky and find Ron. I know what I'd rather do'.

'He's right' said Julie. 'What have we got to lose?'

Randy still wasn't happy. 'What about Ruby? We still haven't found her'.

'Who's Ruby?' asked Julie.

'I forgot to tell you. Ruby is Randy's little sister. said Zak. 'I've not met her, but apparently she went out skating this morning and Randy hasn't seen her since'.

All the blood rushed from Julie's face and she visibly paled. She quickly turned away before Randy could see. Zak noticed though and he turned back to the boy.

'She might have been caught by Ron' he said. 'If we can find him, we'll probably find Ruby too. Worst case, we can use his surveillance system to help?'.

He made a mental note to ask Julie about the girl as soon as he could. He feared the worst. The look on Julie's face said it all. Luckily, Randy had missed it.

'OK' said Randy. 'I hope you're right though. I wouldn't like her to be left alone all night out here'.

Zak threw a warning glance at Julie and she got the message. She wouldn't mention the girl until the time was right.

'Let's go' said Zak getting up. 'It's not far from here is it?'

'No' said Randy. 'These woods will come out near the garden'.

Julie recognised the garden as soon as she saw it. She couldn't believe there was an underground complex beneath.

'This is where I woke up' she said. 'I walked through here this morning. The pond was full then'.

Zak grinned. He wished he could have seen Ron's face when he'd destroyed his treasured fish tank. They crossed the bridge and headed for the hole in the middle of the pond. Zak peered down. It was still a mess. They hadn't got around to tidying it up yet. The floor below still had about an inch of water on it. It was littered with fish, some of the smaller ones still flapping about, while the larger ones stared wide eyed back at him, completely motionless. Sorry guys, thought Zak looking at the casualties he'd caused.

He walked around the edge of the hole, looking into the rooms below to make sure there was nobody around. The door into the corridor had been left open by the guards who had burst in while Zak was escaping.

'We'll go down through the hole' said Zak, 'and then along the corridor. We'll have to make the rest up as we go along'.

'Good plan' said Julie sarcastically. 'I'm so glad I was found by you two'.

She smiled as Zak laughed. 'I'll go first' he said. 'Then I can help you two down. It's quite a drop'.

Julie looked at him offended, pushed past him and jumped deftly into the room below, closely followed by Randy. Zak was left looking sheepishly down at them.

'Do you need a hand?' said Julie, holding hers up and smiling sweetly. 'Wouldn't want you to hurt yourself'.

'I'll bite my tongue next time', he muttered, and dropped down through the hole.

****

The corridor turned to the left at the end and presented them with a security door. Zak retrieved Briggs' pass card from the pocket of his wet jeans. He had been carrying the clothes bag for ages and he thought it seemed unnecessary now they were inside. He made a mental note to dump it when he found a suitable place.

He found a slot in the wall and tried the card. The door beeped politely and slid aside. Another corridor. There were six doors on the right-hand wall and another six on the left.

'Take your pick' said Zak to Julie with a grin. 'I can blame you then if you pick something bad'.

'This plan just gets better and better' said Julie. 'Phase one. Follow your nose. Phase two. Let the woman make the important decisions'.

Zak laughed. He was enjoying Julie's company. Randy had been a little moody, and not much of a conversationalist, so Julie's humour and sarcastic remarks were a breath of fresh air.

'Might as well try that one' she said indicating the nearest door.

Zak grabbed the light gun before inserting his card into the slot by the door. It might fool a guard from a distance, he thought. The door slid aside, and Zak quickly glanced around the doorframe.

The room was empty. Four blank walls stared back at him. He lowered the gun and stepped in, closely followed by Julie and Randy. It wasn't a very big room, maybe eight-foot square, but it seemed bigger due to its emptiness. In the middle of the empty room was a hole in the floor. The hole wasn't empty. It contained a glass ball, about the size of a football. The ball was sat upon a long, vertical rod that split to the left and right about three foot down.

He reached out and touched it, and it lit up and pulsed through a variety of colours. He snatched his hand back, alarmed and the ball returned to its normal clear state.

'What is it?' whispered Julie in awe.

'Crystal ball?' said Zak. 'You're going to meet a tall dark stranger'.

'I've already done that' mumbled Julie. She reached out and touched the surface of the ball and it lit up again. Green, Blue, Red, Orange, Purple, Yellow, Pink. It seemed to fade from one colour to the next, shining brightly on each one before merging to the next. She removed her hand.

'Weird' she said as Randy had a go. He was fascinated.

'Let's try another room' said Zak. 'We might find something to explain it'.

The room opposite was exactly the same. So were the next two.

'What a waste of space' said Randy. 'All of these rooms taken up by little glass balls that light up. What possible use could they have?'

Zak had seen plenty of strange things lately, but he had to agree that this topped everything.

'Have you seen anything strange today?' Zak asked Julie as they worked their way along the other rooms. 'You haven't told us how you got here yet'.

Julie relayed her story to Zak and Randy, leaving out the bit about the girl that must have been Ruby. When she had finished, they had tried eleven of the twelve doors and found the same thing in each one.

'It seems that Ron's been playing games with you as well' said Zak. 'I wonder where the dog went. We never saw him at the fair'.

Julie had completely forgotten about Humbug until she started telling her story. She hoped he was OK. Probably saw a rabbit and gave chase, she thought.

Zak swiped the card for the final door and strolled in as the door slid back.

'What a surprise' he said. 'One hole. One glass, flashy ball thing'.

'And one door' said Julie pointing to the far wall.

Zak blinked in surprise. The expectation of the room being exactly the same had been so great that he hadn't even seen the door at the back of the room. They walked towards it and Zak got his gun ready again.

As the door slid back, all the lights went out.

Chapter 21 – "Irritating little bastard'

Four words flashed through Zak's mind – "They know we're here". He pulled the trigger on the gun and the beam of light pierced the darkness. It didn't give much light, but he was able to see that the new room was much larger than the previous ones had been. He felt Julie grab at him blindly.

'What happened?' There was panic in her voice.

They know we're here. He didn't say it aloud. The words burnt on his brain screaming soundlessly at him.

'Stay together' he ordered. 'Randy. Where are you?'

The boy didn't answer. Julie reached behind her; arms stretched out.

'Randy?' she said, walking back. Zak swung the gun around so she could see better, grabbing at her so that he wouldn't lose her too.

Suddenly, the lights came back on, temporarily blinding them both. It had only been dark for about ten seconds. Randy had gone.

****

Julie and Zak checked the corridor and all the rooms again, but Randy was nowhere to be seen.

'How can he just disappear?' said Julie. 'Even if he decided to run away, he couldn't have got far without your card'.

Zak agreed. He must have been snatched by someone, but how did they take him so quickly and so quietly. He finally voiced the words that had been bugging him.

'They know we're here' he said. 'Why they only grabbed Randy and left us alone I don't know. Perhaps they've taken him to see Ruby'.

'No' said Julie quietly. 'Ruby's dead'.

She told Zak of her encounter with the young girl. It helped to tell somebody else. She had been bottling it up since it had happened, trying to forget about it. When she had finished, she collapsed to the ground and burst into tears, partly because she was so relieved that she had shared it with Zak. He hugged her and did his best to comfort her. He thought he'd been through a lot, but Julie had obviously had a far more harrowing day than he had.

It took her a few minutes to recover her composure, but she finally wiped her eyes and tried to smile. She felt much better. After the long day on her own, she took great comfort in having Zak to lean on.

'So, what do we do now?' she said. 'I'm surprised they haven't come for us yet. They clearly know we're here'.

'It does seem strange' said Zak helping Julie to her feet. I suppose we'd better carry on as before and see what happens. If they do know we're here, I think we'll be led through the complex under their terms'.

They went back to the larger room that they had only seen under torchlight and stared in disbelief. The room was completely empty except for a table and two chairs. The table was set for dinner, a single candle waiting to be lit stood between the two place settings, a casserole bowl and two plates. Zak lifted the lid on the casserole dish and steam wafted out bringing the fresh smell of beef stew with it. It couldn't have been there for more than five minutes.

'OK Ron. I know you're there. Shouldn't you introduce yourself to Julie now. I thought you liked to be polite'. Zak was completely deflated. Ron had been one step ahead of him all the time.

'You're so right Mr McDonald. Good even Miss Morris. I'm so glad to make your acquaintance. We didn't get chance to talk properly earlier'. Ron's mocking voice made Julie shiver. Even when he was talking pleasantly, she could tell that it had been him laughing at her on the phone earlier that day.

'What do you want from us you bastard' she said angrily, looking around, expecting Ron to appear.

Zak pointed her towards the camera he had spotted in the corner of the room. A feeling of déjà vu swept over him.

'I would like you to have an enjoyable meal' said Ron. 'I'm sure you haven't eaten properly all day. You'll feel much less volatile with some decent food inside you'.

Julie rushed toward the table, intending to overturn it and show Run what she thought of his dinner, but Zak stopped her.

'It won't help' he said mournfully. 'Besides. The food looks good. I could really eat now. I'm starving'.

'How can you eat his food' she screamed, her eyes blazing angrily. 'After what he's put us through today. I'd rather stuff it up his...'

'Miss Morris. Miss Morris' said Ron cutting her off. 'You should listen to my friend Zak. He's being very sensible. That's why we get on so well'.

Zak grabbed the lid of the casserole dish and threw it violently at the camera putting a large crack across the lens.

'Listen Ron. Let's get one thing straight. I never was, and never will be any kind of friend of yours. If you ever make an appearance near me, I'll tear your eyes from your head and feed them to your fish'. Zak was suddenly as mad as Julie. 'If there's any left', he added.

Ron laughed and Julie shivered again.

'Eat some food. Both of you. You'll feel much better if you do. It might help to calm you down. I'll check on you in half an hour, after I've been to see my son Randy'.

Zak's mouth dropped open. 'You're son? No way. He helped me to escape'.

'Randy's very good at his job, isn't he? I could put him on the stage if I wanted to. His acting abilities amaze even me sometimes. Have a good meal'. The intercom clicked off.

'I don't believe it' said Zak. 'He must by lying. Randy told me all about his mother and how much he hated this place. He couldn't be working with Ron'. He thought about the day he had spent with the boy but couldn't come up with anything that linked him to Ron. 'He even had a bed in the church. He was living up there. I can't believe the whole thing was a setup to bring me back here. It doesn't make sense'.

'It would explain how he vanished' said Julie as she sat down on one of the chairs. 'And this food. Ron must have known we were coming to get this ready on time'.

'Yes. But it was my idea to come back. Randy tried to put me off, remember? It was as if he was trying to protect me. Not the opposite'.

'It could have been a very good bit of acting. If it was, he certainly convinced me. I would never have guessed'. Julie helped herself to some of the stew. Despite her anger at Ron, she realised that she was hungry too.

'I still don't believe it' said Zak defiantly. 'Ron's just fucking with us. I refuse to believe it until I hear it from the boy himself'.

Zak was angry. He was angry at Ron. He was angry at Randy, and he was angry at himself because part of him did see that he could have been fooled by the boy.

'Forget Randy' said Julie, reaching across the table and placing her hand on Zak's to calm him down. 'Eat some food. You can't do anything about it so there's no point in getting worked up over it'. Julie's rage had subsided fairly quickly. She hadn't spent all day with the boy like Zak had, so her anger was only directed towards Ron.

Zak slowly calmed down and spooned some of the casserole onto his plate. There was a bottle of wine in a bucket of ice at the side of the table and he poured himself a large glass. Julie declined, but Zak poured her some anyway,

'It will do us both good' he said.

They finished the meal in silence, both lost in their own thoughts. Finally, Julie spoke.

'I don't suppose we can just walk out through the pond again. I mean, we've still got the card. What's stopping us?'

'He's probably planted a hundred and one guards there by now' replied Zak. 'Or locked the door. At least we've got each other for company'.

'Yes' said Julie. 'I'm glad you found me. If I'm going to be kidnapped, I'd rather have someone with me to relieve the boredom'.

'Is that all I'm good for' said Zak with a smile. 'To relieve the boredom. What do you want me to do? Sing a song?'

Julie laughed. 'I'll let you know when I need to be serenaded' she said.

'I could provide you with some music if you like?' said Ron unexpectedly, making them both jump. 'A string quartet perhaps?'

'Cut the bullshit Ron. What do you want?' said Zak wearily. He had had a very long day and it was beginning to show.

'I thought I'd have a question and answer session before bed' said Ron cheerfully. 'You ask me any question and I'll do my best to answer it'. He laughed. 'Well, I might' he added.

'Why are you such an irritating little bastard?' asked Julie.

Zak burst out laughing. 'Answer that one if you can' he said.

'I wouldn't waste the opportunity' said Ron grimly. 'I may not be feeling so generous tomorrow'.

Julie pulled a face at the camera which set Zak off laughing again.

'OK Ron'. Said Zak at last. 'Why are we here? You could at least tell us that'.

'You are here to participate in an experiment' said Ron brightly.

Zak waited for more, but nothing came. 'That's it? It's a bit vague isn't it. Can't you tell us more?'

'I'll tell you more when the experiment is ready' said Ron.

'Is it dangerous?'

'No. Not at all'.

'Why us. Why are we involved?'

'I believe that nobody else will be able to give me the result that I want' said Ron.

Why have you been tormenting us all day?' said Julie.

'Because it was necessary' said Ron. 'It's connected with the experiment'.

'This is bullshit' shouted Zak suddenly. 'You're not giving us answers. You're avoiding the questions. You sound like a politician'.

Ron laughed. 'I can assure you I am not. Any more questions?'

'Was Ruby meant to die?' said Julie quietly.

'An unfortunate accident' said Ron sadly. 'I promise you that you weren't supposed to see that. It was a matter of being in the wrong place at the wrong time'.

'What was the piece of glass doing across the road like that?'

'The whole complex is surrounded by glass. It's the boundary wall'.

'Why glass?' asked Zak.

'Why not?' answered Ron.

'How long are you going to keep us for?'

'As long as the experiment lasts'.

'And what happens to us then?' said Julie. 'Will you let us go after the experiment?'

Ron didn't answer.

'Will you let us go after the experiment?' Julie repeated, raising her voice.

'I think it's time for bed' said Ron. A door at the back of the room slid open. 'Have a good rest. I'll speak to you in the morning'.

'Bastard' whispered Julie.

Chapter 22 – "Ventilation"

Despite their anger at Ron, the bedroom was inviting. It was furnished in much the same way as the house above that Julie had woken up in. The room seemed out of place compared to the others with their plain walls and unfurnished décor.

'Do you think he's telling the truth?' said Julie as she lay back on one of the twin beds, staring at the ceiling. 'About the experiment I mean. It's a bit weird isn't it? What have we got that's so special?'

Zak was pacing the room looking for any secret doors or passages. With his previous experience in the complex, he knew that such things could easily be hidden.

'I don't know' he said, examining the wall beside her bed. 'I think his explanation is a bit too unclear to read anything in to. I wouldn't believe anything one hundred per cent if I were you'. He stood on her bed and reached up towards a metal grid that was screwed to the wall about a foot below the ceiling.

'You're probably right. What are you up to?'. She sat up to avoid his feet. 'What's that?'

'Not sure. It looks like it's there for ventilation, but I can't see properly'. He jumped off the bed and dragged it out of the way and grabbed at a dressing table 'Here. Help me with this?'.

She helped him drag the dressing table across the room until it was below the grid. They both climbed up and peered through the many holes. There wasn't much to see.

'I think you're right. Ventilation' said Julie, jumping down again. 'The air's got to get in here somehow'.

'I'm not sure' said Zak, retrieving the gun and shooting the light through the holes. 'There's no breeze coming through here. If it was linked either to a ventilation system or directly outside, there would be something'.

The beam from the gun shone through, but he couldn't make anything out.

'Can't see a thing' he said. He jumped down. 'Probably worth a closer look though'. He went back to the room next door and grabbed a knife off of his dinner plate and returned to the dressing table. Using the blade of the knife as a screwdriver, he worked at the four screws holding the grid to the wall.

'Couldn't we just smash it somehow?' said Julie scanning the room for something heavy. 'It doesn't look very strong. We can pretend it's Ron's face'.

'Ha ha. Don't tempt me' said Zak. 'Have a look in the drawers'. He was struggling with the first screw. 'If you can find a better screwdriver it would help'.

Julie searched the room but came up empty handed. 'There's not much here' she said. 'Just the usual stuff. Not many people keep tools in the bedroom'.

'I had an uncle once who used to hang all his tools in the bedroom cupboard' said Zak, starting on the second screw. 'Auntie Mo was always moaning at him. Said that she wanted the space to hang her clothes. He secretly called her Auntie Moaner'.

Julie laughed. 'I don't blame her. Did he move them?'

'No. He built her another cupboard. Using his tools'.

'I'm surprised she put up with him' said Julie, 'Wouldn't it have been easier to put the tools elsewhere?'

'That's what everybody said. Especially when she left him'.

'She left him. Just because of that?'

'No. She caught him with another woman'.

'Is there a point to this story?' said Julie exasperated. 'What had the other woman got to do with his tool cupboard?'

Zak rested as the second screw dropped to the ground and he turned back to Julie with a grin.

'Auntie Mo caught him trying to get the other woman to hide in the cupboard. The tool cupboard'.

Julie laughed again. 'I don't believe that. You're making it up'.

'It's true' said Zak. 'Apparently, the woman was complaining because his spanner collection was digging into her bare flesh. Auntie Mo hit the roof. So did most of the tools by the time she had finished' he added. He turned back to the grid and started on the next screw.

Julie looked at him, half shocked, half smiling. Was this a true story? She wasn't convinced.

'I'll take your word for it' she said.

She didn't see him trying to stop himself from laughing as the third screw dropped and the metal grid swung down, pivoting on the last one.

'We're in' he said tossing the knife to the floor. 'Do you want to go first?'

'You don't really believe that we're going to be able to get through that do you?' said Julie. 'It's too small. We'll get stuck. We don't even know if it leads anywhere'.

She tried to think up more excuses but couldn't come up with anything convincing. Zak hoisted himself up by his fingers and peered into the gap that he had just uncovered.

'If my shoulders will go through then the rest will follow' he said. 'You're much smaller than me so you shouldn't have any problems'.

'You aren't joking, are you? What are you hoping to achieve? I expect we're being watched as we speak'.

'What have we got to lose? Said Zak with a shrug.

'Flesh' said Julie. 'Mainly from the upper arms'.

Zak laughed. 'Well, things have certainly become more fun since I met you' he said sarcastically. 'I'm gonna start calling you Mo. Wouldn't you rather be escaping than stuck in a small room with nothing but a bed?'

'I'd rather be in the ghost train' said Julie under her breath. 'At least it was spacious'.

Zak laughed but wouldn't be deterred. 'Come on. I'll help you up. You better go first. You won't be able to reach it without my help'.

Julie was stood with her hands on her hips, glaring at him but she couldn't stop herself from smiling. She climbed up next to him, and they counted to three and Julie jumped as Zak lifted her to the hole above. She gripped the sides.

'Christ you're heavy' said Zak. 'How much of that casserole did you eat?'

'Watch it' said Julie. 'I may be smaller than you, but I can still kick pretty hard'. Her feet were swinging wildly near his head as she wriggled forward on her belly until she was fully into the hole.

'What now?' she shouted, her voice echoing back towards Zak.

'Now I put the grid back' Zak shouted back. 'Move your feet'.

'Don't you dare' she said laughing. 'Where's the light gun? I can't see a bloody thing'.

Zak had it in his hand and was about to pass it up. 'Err. Don't know' he said. 'Can't you just feel around a bit. See what you can find?'

'Brilliant' she said to herself as she wriggled forward. 'I'll probably find a dead end. Or a twenty-foot drop'.

Zak pulled himself up as Julie's feet vanished and followed her into the hole. He pulled the trigger on the gun.

'Oh look. I've found the torch' he said. 'At least I can see'.

'You know, you must be the kindest, most generous man that I've ever met' said Julie with as much sarcasm as she could muster. 'Do you take after your uncle?'

'I haven't got an uncle' said Zak innocently.

'You shit' she screamed. I can't believe I fell for that stupid story.

Zak laughed and bumped into Julie's feet where she had stopped.

'Keep moving Mo or I'll bite your ankles' he said chuckling. 'Did I tell you about my great grandmother Nellie? She had her ankles bitten off by a goat'.

'I'm not listening to you anymore' said Julie shuffling forward again 'Oww'.

'What's wrong?' said Zak.

'I just hit my head' she said.

That started Zak off laughing again and she kicked out, cracking him on the nose.

'Alright, alright' he said trying to compose himself and ducking from her flying feet. 'What have you hit? Is it the end of the road?'

'Looks like another grid' she said peering through the small holes that were in it. 'I can't see much though. The holes are slanted upwards. I can only see the roof'.

'Let's have a look. Move to the left a bit. Budge up'.

'Can you be serious for five minutes?' said Julie. 'See if you can pass me the torch. I might be able to see something with it'.

She reached back the best she could and just managed to stretch her hand back. Zak passed her the gun and she pulled the trigger lighting up the grid in front of her. The light made her realise how narrow the passage was and she suddenly began to feel very claustrophobic.

'It's not helping' she said. 'We'll have to go back. I want to get out of here'.

Zak could hear the slight panic in her voice.

'Are you OK?' he said, genuinely concerned.

'I'll be alright' she said. 'Let's just go back. You can try again. Feet first if you can. See if you can smash your way through the grid.

Zak shuffled back as quick as he could. He had to admit that the tunnel was very restricting, and the air was becoming difficult to breathe as they used the oxygen up. He jumped out and lifted her gently back down. The colour had drained from her face and she was quite shaky.

'Are you sure you're OK?' said Zak. 'You look a bit pale'.

She smiled. 'Better now' she said. 'Things were closing in on me a bit in there. The shadows from the torch didn't help'.

'I know what you mean' he said. 'Have a lie down. I'll go back and work on that grid'.

He jumped up and into the tunnel but came back straight away.

'I don't suppose you can help me first?' he said as she was lying back. 'I can't turn in the tunnel. Can you help me get in the other way around?'

'Nope. You're on your own' she said, sticking her nose in the air in a mock gesture. 'And you're not taking this'. She lunged forward and grabbed the gun from him.

'And I was genuinely concerned for you' said Zak with a laugh. 'What a faker'.

'I'm a very sick woman' Julie said holding her hand to her head. 'I need my rest'.

Zak grabbed her and pulled her up.

'Sick in the head perhaps' he said. 'You can rest after helping me up'.

****

He reached the end of the tunnel again and rested before kicking out hard at the grid with his feet.

'Keep the noise down dear. I've got a headache' called Julie from the distance.

He grinned. Meeting Julie had been the only pleasant thing that had happened all day. He was almost glad he'd been kidnapped.

It took six hefty kicks before the screws holding the grid in place snapped and it went crashing to the floor. Hope there's nobody in there, he thought. Would've scared the life out of them. He backed down the tunnel again and crawled out headfirst on to the dressing table. He didn't fancy launching himself out the other end without being able to see what was there. He'd tried that trick once already today, he mused remembering throwing himself blindly off the bed that morning. Had it really been the same day?

'Back so soon?' said Julie. 'I was hoping for another twenty minutes kip at least. The neighbours are awfully noisy tonight. So hard to get any rest'.

'Let's go and sort them out then' said Zak. 'After you'.

'What a gentleman'.

Chapter 23 – "Speedy"

'Welcome to the East wing' said Julie as Zak jumped down behind her.

'It's not as nice as the West is it?' he said, looking around the dreary room they had entered. 'We really must have words with the cleaner'.

The room was much smaller than the bedroom and the décor wasn't very pretty. The walls were painted in a sickly yellow colour, but the paint had faded so it made the room look dull rather than brightening it up. It was difficult to say what the purpose of the room was, as all it contained was the bent-up grid that Zak had smashed through.

'At least it's got a door' said Julie. 'If that doesn't work, I'm going straight back to my bed next door'.

There was no slot for Zak to put his card in. It wasn't even a sliding door like the others had been. It was like any other normal door with a handle on it.

He tried it.

It opened.

He peered out.

He closed it again.

'It's a cupboard' he said. 'Is it the only door?'

'I hope you're joking' said Julie grabbing the handle and yanking the door open as Zak chuckled. She peered outside and jumped in horror.

The passageway that she was looking into was like any other passageway. It was long. It had doors. It even had a small sign that read "Passageway B2". The only unusual thing about it was the small robot that was hurtling towards her at high speed. Before she had time to jump back and slam the door, the robot

– which turned out to be a tortoise on wheels – shot past her launching a small glass ball as it passed. Zak heard Julie gasp and jumped forward, just in time to see the fastest tortoise he'd ever seen shoot past. He saw the small glass ball flying through the air towards them and grabbed Julie, throwing her to the floor. The glass shattered as he threw himself on top of her, anticipating the explosion.

It came. The lower part of his left leg was briefly engulfed in flames, singeing his blistered foot and burning the hairs on his ankle to a crisp. His scream rang through the empty room, just inches from Julie. She crawled out from under Zak, clutching her left ear as the noise bounced around her head. She slammed the door and turned to see the damage.

The bomb had actually missed Zak's leg. If it had caught it, she would probably be looking at a scorched stump. The flames had burnt out already and at first glance it didn't look too bad. She carefully peeled off the oversized shoe that he had pinched from Briggs earlier and removed the sock.

The shoe had taken a lot of the heat away from his foot, but his ankle hadn't been so lucky. There were large red sores beginning to appear around it and it looked very tender.

'How bad is it?' she asked, glancing around the room in the vain hope that she might find something, anything that might help to ease the pain.

'Not good' said Zak. The sudden shock and burst of pain had taken his breath from him and he almost panted the words out. 'It stings like hell'.

'There's no water' said Julie. 'There's nothing in this room at all'.

'Don't worry. It will be better in a minute. Once the shock has worn off'.

'You need cold water on it'. She got up. I'll go back to the bedroom. There might be something in there. Some cream or something at least'.

'No. It's OK'. His breath was returning to normal, but he was still wincing in pain. 'Are you alright?'

'I can't believe you're worried about me' said Julie. 'You almost had your foot blown off and you ask if I'm OK?'. The shock of the incident had just caught up with her. She realised that if Zak hadn't dragged her out of the way, it would have been her lying in agony, probably a lot worse. She sat down next to him and examined his ankle again.

'Can you move it?' she asked. He tried and found that he could but not without a stab of pain.

'I can, but I'd rather not' he said. 'What the hell was that? Looked like a tortoise on speed'. He laughed, but it turned into moans of pain as the laughter rocked his body and moved his ankle.

Julie got up. 'Ron? Are you there Ron?' she shouted.

'What are you doing?' said Zak alarmed.

'You need help' said Julie. 'I can't help you in here. Ron may be a bastard but if he needs you for an experiment then he'll help you. Give you a painkiller or something. At least some cold water'.

'I don't want help from him' said Zak defiantly. 'We've got his far. We can't give in now'.

'But we can't go on with you like that' said Julie. 'Besides. We're trapped I'm not going out there with Speedy waiting for me'.

Zak smiled. The pain was easing slightly. 'Get the gun' he said. 'If you shoot it in the right place it will probably kill it'.

'Probably? That's a long shot. That things lethal'.

'I'll do it then' said Zak, starting to hoist himself up, trying to ignore the fresh pain that shot through his foot. He got to one knee before she stopped him.

'Don't be silly. You won't be able to jump out the way again if you miss'. She grabbed the gun from him. 'I'll see what I can do'.

'Julie?'

She looked at him.

'Be careful' he said. Julie bent down and kissed him gently, taking him by surprise. A nice surprise, he thought.

'Don't worry' she said. 'Even I'm faster than a tortoise'.

****

Zak crawled behind the door as Julie opened it a crack and peered out. There was no sign of Speedy so she opened the door wider and looked both ways.

'Where are you, you miserable creature' she murmured under her breath.

She was answered by a whirring sound coming towards her from the end of the corridor. She trained the gun on the tortoise and pulled the trigger. The beam of light wasn't strong enough to reach it at this range, but it was closing fast. As it got nearer, she could see a round patch of glass between its eyes and guessed that this was her target. She moved the light beam slowly towards it.

The tortoise dodged. She blinked in surprise. Did I imagine that? She tried again but the same thing happened. The tortoise distinctly moved a few inches to the right. It was almost on top of her now and she could see the glass ball sitting on its back waiting to be launched. She let out a cry, and threw herself backwards, slamming the door behind her.

The wooden door shook in its frame as it took the blast. A hole appeared in the middle about the size of a fist, smoke drifting from it, splinters of wood spraying over them both. She got up and dusted herself down.

'Did you miss?' asked Zak.

'Bloody thing ducked' she said. 'I'll get in next time'.

'I wasn't joking when I said be careful' said Zak.

'And I wasn't joking when I said I'll get it next time' replied Julie grimly. She bent and picked up the metal grill.

'What are you going to do? Beat it to death?'

She smiled. 'You can watch if you like' she said. 'Here. Hold this'. She passed him the gun and opened the door again.

'Are you crazy?' said Zak dragging himself towards her. He reached the door and stuck the top of his body out around her legs, reaching forward with the gun to take aim.

Speedy was coming back. He could see him in the distance approaching fast.

'Get back' screamed Julie. 'I can't do this with you there'.

'Do what?' said Zak.

'Never mind. Just get back'.

Zak ignored her and he pulled the trigger, taking aim at the closing-in robot. The light fell a bit low. He lifted slightly, and just as he thought he was bang on the tortoise dodged.

'Are you happy now?' screamed Julie. 'Get out of the bloody way. I can't drag us both back when the next bomb blows'.

Zak had one more attempt but realised that Julie was right. He tried to slide backwards, but knocked his ankle on the floor, momentarily halting him as the pain flared up.

'Move' said Julie, and then again more urgently. 'Move. Go. Now'.

Zak scrambled back, ignoring the pain now. He could see Speedy out of the corner of his eye and he knew he only had about a second before the bomb was launched.

Julie launched first. She threw the metal grid a fraction before the bomb came towards her and leapt back with a scream. The grid met the bomb in mid-air, and both came crashing down on Speedy's head. Julie tripped over Zak and fell towards the floor as the bomb blew, causing Speedy to hit the roof in a shower of sparks and flames. The metal grid was blown back towards the door and hurtled towards Julie as she tumbled.

Zak caught her and cushioned most of the impact of her fall. The grid sailed over her head, missing by less than an inch, and crashed to the floor behind them. They lay where they were for several long seconds, arms entwined around each other getting their breath back. Their eyes locked for a second.

'Good shot' said Zak.

Chapter 24 – "Static Electricity"

Julie help Zak along the passageway but it was fairly slow going. He found that he had problems putting too much weight on his damaged ankle so was relying on Julie to be a prop.

'I still think we should call Ron for help' she said. 'What on Earth are we going to do if another tortoise takes a pot shot at us?'

'That's not a sentence you hear every day' laughed Zak. 'I don't think there will be another. It would have shown up by now. Anyway. I'd put money on the fact that Ron's watching us all the time. Probably having a good laugh at our expense'.

'But he could have killed you. Or me. What good would we be to him then?'

'The explosive wasn't strong enough to do any serious damage. It's probably a warning to stop us from wandering around. I'd rather stay on the move, even if we get nowhere. I get a great sense of enjoyment by doing the opposite of what Ron wants'.

'So – you're a rebel? He's a dangerous man to get on the wrong side of' said Julie gravely. 'You know he could kill us if he wanted to'.

'Exactly. Yet we're still alive' said Zak. 'If he wanted us dead then we'd have been dead a long time ago. Perhaps there's a little bit of truth in his "experiment" explanation'.

'I'm not convinced' said Julie. 'Perhaps we'll find out more if we just do as he says'.

Zak stopped as they came to a door in the passageway. 'But that's boring' he replied with a grin. 'Where's your sense of fun? At least it gives us something to do while we wait for him to fill us in. And if it annoys Ron, then as far as I'm concerned it's worthwhile'.

He inserted his pass card in the hole in the wall and the door slide aside.

'Still works' he said surprised.

The room was the same as all the others that they had seen earlier in the previous corridor. The strange crystal ball that lit up when it was touched. The rod connecting to the ball from below.

'I wonder if they're all linked?' said Julie. 'The rods joining together underground. What's it for though?'

'Beats me' said Zak. 'This whole place is too strange to speculate on what it is. Or what it used to be. I assume the world above us was used at some point. I mean – The church, the fairground, the beach. They must have emptied the whole town. What happened to all the people?'

'I hadn't thought of that' said Julie. She stopped. Something was bugging her, and she frowned. 'There was something else unusual about it. Did you see any houses? I mean, where people might have lived? I can't remember seeing anything like that, except for the one where I woke up – and that was only a room' she added.

'No. You're right' said Zak. 'Perhaps they had everything knocked down. I can't think of a good reason why though'.

They turned to leave the strange room when suddenly, the ball in the middle of the room lit up a bright blue. As they watched it, it changed to green. Then yellow. And soon it was showing off its display of many colours, rotating through them slowly at first, and then faster.

'What's it doing?' whispered Julie.

Zak shrugged. He kept his eyes locked on the sphere in the centre of the room, almost afraid to take his eyes away in case he missed something.

Suddenly, the ball shone a bright red and a loud hum filled the room. The hum was quickly followed by a static charge that filled the air around them. They could feel the hair on their heads and arms being pulled towards the centre of the room. It grew stronger, and Julie winced as it tugged at the roots on her scalp. She stepped back out of the door, trying to drag Zak with her, but the light show had momentarily paralysed him.

'Zak' she shouted over the buzzing sound. 'Come on. What are you waiting for?'.

He shook his head, releasing himself from his trance, and stepped back just as everything stopped. He felt his hair drop back into place as the charge eased. The hum didn't die down slowly, but just cut off abruptly. One second it was as if there were a thousand bees in the tiny room. The next second it was silent.

Julie broke the silence. 'What...'.

She didn't get a chance to finish. The ball exploded. There was no warning No bright lights. No sound. It just blew apart, the glass scattering outward, millions of tiny splinters of glass hurtled towards them at alarming speed. Just as the first pieces of glass reached them, the door slid neatly back into place.

Julie screamed and held her hands up, an instant reaction to what was coming at her. It hadn't registered that the door had slid back and was shielding them.

Zak stumbled back too, a burst of pain shooting through his ankle, causing him to cry out in unison with Julie. A second passed before they realised what had happened and another second before they realised they were both unhurt.

Julie tried again. 'What was that? That charge? It was pulling me. Pulling me towards...'

'I know' said Zak. 'I felt it too. It was electrical. It must have built up the static to such a degree that it was pulling us in. Probably caused the ball to explode too'.

'Do you think they all did this?' said Julie, wide eyed. 'There's lots of them. I wonder if they all exploded?'

'I don't know. Maybe. Let's have a look'.

They crossed the passageway to the opposite room and looked in. There was no disturbance, but the feeling of static electricity was still apparent in the air.

'Whatever we just saw, it was extremely powerful' said Zak. 'If all of these crystal balls produced the same energy that we just experienced, there would be enough power to light up the whole town'.

'Perhaps that's it' said Julie. 'Perhaps it's some kind of energy source. A generator maybe? Ron said that we were involved in an experiment. What's to say that there isn't more than one going on'.

'It's possible' said Zak doubtfully. 'Strangest damn generator I've ever seen though'.

Julie nodded. They turned away from the room, Zak leaning on Julie for support and looked back up the corridor.

'OK. You're right. This is pointless' he said eventually. 'We're not going to escape tonight. Not with my ankle like this. We might as well go back and have a good night's sleep. At least we'll be refreshed for the morning'.

'That's the best idea you've had all day' said Julie with a smile. 'Did a piece of glass whack you in the head and knock some sense into you?'

He laughed. 'Come on. Let's get back to the bedroom'.

The latest incident had worried Zak. He kept picturing what would have happened if the door hadn't shut just at the right moment. The glass pieces could have seriously hurt them both. He found he was more anxious about protecting Julie than he was for himself. He had grown very fond of her in the short time that they had been together and didn't feel that he could protect her properly with his ankle the way it was.

As Julie led him along the corridor, Zak suddenly stopped.

'Umm. How are we going to get back into the hatch? We have no dressing table to stand on, and my foot has seen better days'.

As if in answer, the door they were passing slid open. They realised it led to the one where they started. The one where Randy had disappeared earlier. The one with the bedroom behind it.

'Bastard' said Zak under his breath. 'I knew he was watching us'.

As he slumped down on the bed, Zak noticed that two tablets had been placed on the side with a glass of water. He took them with a quick swallow. It wasn't long before the painkiller set in and he drifted into a deep sleep.

****

He woke several hours later and was surprised and pleased to find Julie cuddled up next to him. He leaned over and kissed her gently and she stirred.

'Sorry. I didn't mean to wake you' he said.

'I'm glad you did' she said, kissing him back. 'How's the foot?'

'A bit better. Better still with you taking my mind off it'.

'Whatever do you mean' she said innocently, her hands running slowly down his body, finding the zip on his shorts.

'I'll let you work it out' he said moaning.

They made love twice, each of them realising that they might not get the chance again and wishing that the circumstances were different. Afterwards, as they lay still in the dark, arms locked together, a sense of serenity swept over Zak. Even if he and Julie didn't get out of this place, at least they had had one night together. It was a bright end to a very traumatic day for them both.

He watched Julie fall asleep, and it wasn't long before is eyes dropped again too.

Chapter 25 – "Ron"

They woke up fairly late, Zak's watch told him that it was 10:30 already. If it wasn't for the watch, they wouldn't have been able to tell whether it was night or day. There were no windows to give them any clues.

They made love again before finally rising, wondering why they hadn't been woken up by Ron earlier.

'He's probably been watching us' grumbled Julie. 'Cheap thrills. Perhaps that's what we're here for'.

'If that's true then I don't really mind' said Zak, dragging himself out of bed. 'There's far worse ways to spend my time'. He carefully put his injured foot on the floor and was surprised that it didn't hurt too much. 'That painkiller must have been strong' he said hobbling across the floor. 'I can almost put my weight on it already'.

'That and my own form of therapeutic remedy' said Julie with a sexy smile. 'Which direction did you fling my bra last night? I can't find it anywhere'.

'You look better without it' said Zak admiring her naked body. 'Leave it off'.

She laughed and scoured the room finally finding it hiding under the dresser. After washing and dressing, they discovered that someone had set up breakfast in the room next door. The candles had been removed along with the leftovers of the casserole from the previous night. In their place was a fried breakfast that made Zak's mouth water just looking at it. Bacon, eggs, sausage, mushrooms, tomatoes, toast and even hash browns. A large pot of tea sat between them and he helped himself.

'Not bad' he said. 'We should come here more often. Do the last two weeks in August work for you?'

'Suits me' said Julie through a mouthful of toast. 'Must remember to pick up a leaflet for my friends'.

'I'll let you have one after breakfast' said Ron suddenly. 'July would be better though. We're doing a family special'.

'I wish you wouldn't just barge in when we're eating' said Julie. 'Didn't your mother ever teach you manners?'

'You're so right' said Ron. 'Please forgive me for interrupting your breakfast. I've got some good news for you though'.

'Let me guess' said Zak. 'You're feeling a bit guilty for putting us through a day of hell and you've decided to let us go?'

'Not quite' replied Ron. 'I'd like to see you after breakfast. Both of you. I'm looking forward to meeting you at last'.

'Not half as much as I'm looking forward to meeting you' mumbled Zak. Ron didn't hear him or chose to ignore him if he did.

'When you are ready, just knock on the outside door and someone will show you the way' said Ron. 'Oh, and don't rush your breakfast on my account. I've got all day'.

There was a click as the intercom was switched off and Julie and Zak were left in silence.

'So, what happens now?' said Julie.

'I guess the experiment starts, whatever it is' said Zak, swigging back his cup of tea. 'I'm ready when you are. If this is what we are here for then I want to get it over and done with as soon as possible. At least we might find out what's going on at last'.

'Maybe' said Julie thoughtfully. 'I can't help feeling a bit scared though'.

'I know what you mean' said Zak. 'But I think last night proved we can't escape. Let's go and see what he wants. Better to go voluntarily. I haven't got the energy to go kicking and screaming. Your fault' he added with a glint in his eye.

'Voluntarily?' said Julie. 'We're hardly getting much of a choice here. If Ron was to open the door and give me a choice, I know which way I'd be going'.

Zak laughed. 'I wouldn't be far behind you' he said. 'Ready?'

'Ready as I'll ever be' she said nervously.

They got up and made for the door. Zak leaned down kissed Julie before hammering on the door with his fist. The door slid back, and they found themselves face to face with three armed guards. They were escorted along the familiar corridors and finally came to a stop by a blank wall with a camera mounted above it. After a couple of seconds, a panel slid back in the wall revealing another corridor. It was so well disguised that Zak couldn't see the join between wall and door when it slid back into place behind him.

The new corridor was much shorter and only had one door in the end. As they approached it, they realised it was actually an elevator. One of the guards pressed the button and the doors slid neatly aside. They all stepped in and a button was pressed causing the lift to go up.

When the lift stopped Zak and Julie were pushed out and the guards descended again, leaving them alone. Before they had a chance to take in their surroundings, a fleet of robots shot towards them and circled them completely. The robots crawled forward, forcing them to walk too. They were led to two chairs in the middle of the room where they sat down. The robots settled quietly around them and appeared to switch off.

'So, what now?' said Julie.

Zak didn't have to answer. A hole appeared in the floor in front of them and a chair slowly rose through it. Like something out of a dodgy sixties spy film, thought Zak. All it needed was some smoke and a fanfare.

Sat on the chair was man of about fifty, slightly balding and more than a few pounds overweight.

'We meet at last' said Ron.

****

Zak leapt up and hobbled towards Ron as fast as his swollen foot would allow. Unfortunately, this wasn't very fast and the robot that was sat between him and Ron suddenly sprang to life and shot Zak. It wasn't a bullet, or a glass bomb – but more a miniature bolt of lightning. A blue line arced from the robot's head and found his shoulder. The shock felt similar to being hit by an iron bar, and he fell to the floor at Julie's feet. The pain subsided immediately, and the robot returned to its spot and sat motionless once again.

'That's probably not a good idea' said Ron getting up and pacing around the robots. 'I have no intention on hurting you Zak. The robots are programmed to shoot only if you break the circle. If you insist on doing it, then you're effectively bringing the pain on to yourself'.

'Cut the crap Ron' said Zak getting up and glaring at him. 'You've had great pleasure trying to inflict pain on me on the last couple of days. I'd hardly call "this" an unintentional injury'. He waved his injured foot towards Ron to show him what he meant, but accidentally broke the circle of robots again. The bolt of lightning struck the foot and he screamed in pain and fell to the floor once again.

Ron chuckled.

'Call these things off' said Julie jumping up. 'Can't you see how much pain he's in already. How can you keep on doing this?'

'It's all self-inflicted my dear' said Ron coolly. 'Stay in the circle and you'll be fine'. He turned to Zak. 'Looks a bit nasty that ankle. I wouldn't recommend doing that too often'.

He turned and sat down on his chair again and became all business-like.

'Please take your seats now. I thought you wanted to know why you were brought here. It's time to tell you a story'.

Julie helped Zak to his chair. His foot hadn't recovered from the blow it had received and a sharp pain shot up his leg each time he put it on the ground making him wince.

'OK Ron' he said once he was sitting. 'What kind of experiment have you got planned for us? It would be nice to know what's going to happen to us before you start prodding and poking'.

'Oh, didn't I tell you?' said Ron with a smile. 'The experiment's finished. You'll be pleased to know that you both passed with flying colours'.

Chapter 26 – "TTT"

Zak and Julie stared at Ron amazed.

'What do you mean? said Julie. 'We haven't done anything'.

'I've been looking forward to this bit' he said. 'You'll have to pay close attention for a while. The explanation I'm about to give you is...how shall we say? – a little complicated'.

'I'm sure we can cope' said Zak. 'Get on with it'.

'OK. Here goes'. He took a deep breath. 'It all started in the year 2009. There was a ….'

'Hang on', interrupted Zak. 'Is this a fairy story? It's only 1994'.

'I did say it was complicated' laughed Ron. 'You'll have to keep an open mind for this. It is possible for this story to begin in the year 2009 for two reasons. Number one – time travel was discovered in that year. And….', he paused for effect. 'Number two - the year isn't 1994 now - It's 2017. You have been brought forward in time to fix an issue caused by a TTT on a routine mission'.

'What's a TTT?' asked Julie. It was the first thing that came into her mind. She hadn't really grasped what Ron had just said.

Zak burst from his chair before she could get an answer. 'What the hell are you waffling on about?' he said angrily. 'Time travel? What planet are you on? This is real life not fantasy. I thought you were perhaps a little bit crazy but now I know that you're completely insane'.

'A TTT' said Ron, ignoring Zak's outburst and turning to Julie, 'is a traveller through time. The first time-travellers were known as "Travellers in Time" but this was changed as the acronym was a bit childish'. He chuckled.

Zak couldn't help himself from laughing.

'I can't believe that you've dragged us up here to tell us all this rubbish' he said. 'What's the point of this exercise? To see which one of us is the most gullible?'

Ron continued to ignore Zak.

'The first TTT was sent back in time to observe a known event, just to prove that it was really working. It was on December 24th 2009, Christmas Eve. I'll never forget it. There was a lottery. All the people that had been working on the project for more than ten years stood a chance of being the one who was chosen to go back'.

Ron sat back in his chair and clasped his fingers together. A look of contentment on his face.

'And I won. I only qualified for the draw by six weeks and I won. There were men and women in that room who had been involved in the project for over twenty-five years, spending seventy-hour weeks slaving over computers to come up with solutions to almost impossible problems. But I was the chosen one. It was me who was the first TTT.

'Fascinating' said Zak. 'Let me guess. They sent you to the loony bin and you only escaped last week'.

Ron turned to Zak at last. 'I get the impression that you don't quite believe everything I'm telling you' he said with a smile.

'You don't say' said Zak.

'Let me ask you a question. Which part don't you believe?'

'Am I supposed to believe any of it?' said Zak amazed. 'Call me stupid if you like, but I don't think it's unreasonable to consider everything you've said as utter bullshit'.

'It's the time travel bit that you can't come to terms with isn't it?' said Ron stating the obvious. 'Think about it for a minute. Do you know how advanced computers have become in the last ten years of your lifetime? Not my lifetime – yours. In the early 1980's, the first home computers were brought to market. Silly little machines that kids used to play Space Invaders and Pac Man on, but it was only the beginning. Just ten years later they were producing computers that made early efforts look like calculators. Smaller, faster machines that could perform thousands, even millions of calculations in the blink of an eye. The exponential growth in the processing power was phenomenal'.

He paused, poured himself a glass of water and continued.

'Then came virtual reality, a computer world to explore. A world that could contain anything that the programmers wanted to put into it. In a short number of years, computers more-or-less took over the world. People were being made redundant as they were replaced by machines that were infinitely more efficient. Wherever you went, there was a computer nearby doing the work of a whole team of people – and quicker'.

'Now, let's project forward a few years. You already know how computers grew in the eighties. What if that same growth rate continued year after year? What next?'

Ron had finally caught Zak's attention and was greeted with a stunned silence.

'I'll tell you. Anything. Anything you can possibly think of will eventually be possible with the aid of a computer. It may take a hundred years of improved technology – probably less in my experience, but it will be possible'.

'But time travel?' said Zak. 'You can't be serious. It just isn't possible'.

'Why not?' said Ron. 'Where there's a problem, there's a computer somewhere that will find you an answer'.

Zak looked at him mystified.

'It didn't just happen out of the blue, I might add' said Ron. 'The project began way back in 1980. The idea was already being prepared then. A brilliant scientist names Robert Gilder realised the potential of the computer and assembled a small team to start working immediately on it. It took sixteen years before technology had advanced enough for his time machine plans to become a viable idea. It was another thirteen years before its completion. Sadly, Robert died in 2005, just four years before his dream, became a reality. Of course, he knows about it now. A TTT was sent back to give him all the details'.

'This is all very enlightening' said Zak. 'But I still don't buy it. I mean – The whole idea of time travel just isn't feasible. There's too many complications'.

'You must remember that Robert had been working on "complications" as you put it, for many many years. He thought of everything. Every possible flaw in the logic of time travel, he found an answer for'.

'Then you can prove it' said Julie suddenly. She hadn't spoken for a while and the two men looked around when she did. 'If we're really in the future, in the year 2017, you should be able to prove it very easily'. She had taken in everything that Ron had said and the concept that she just couldn't grasp was that they were over twenty years in the future.

'I'm surprised that you're both finding this so hard to accept', said Ron tiredly. 'Look at this'. He pointed to one of the robots that sat patiently at his feet, daring someone to cross its path.

'Do you think that robots such as these were this advanced in the 1990's? These things know where you are. They have artificial intelligence. They can distinguish you from the rest of the room. They can tune in to sounds beyond human frequencies. You could hide in the corner of a pitch-black room and this thing could tune in to your breathing. And - they work together. Their self-awareness is mind boggling. This model was created in 2016. It's only a year old'.

'It's hardly conclusive proof' said Julie, but she sounded doubtful. She certainly hadn't seen anything like these robots before. 'If we assume that everything you're saying is true, that time travel is possible, and that we've been brought forwards to 2017, then what's it all about? Where do we fit into this?'

'I can only get to that part when you accept that everything I have told you is true' said Ron. 'I haven't even got to the confusing part yet. If you don't believe me now, then you never will'.

'OK. I'm not convinced' said Zak impatiently. 'Yes – The robots are impressive, but it's still too sci-fi for me to accept. But, for the purposes of this conversation I'll willing to believe you. Tell us the rest of your little story and maybe we can all go home'. He didn't believe a word of it. Ron was obviously a fruitcake and the only way to find out why they were here was to humour him.

Ron laughed. 'I'll carry on' he said. 'But please remember to keep an open mind. I haven't told you any lies, you know. All of this fact'.

Zak grunted in disagreement, but he said nothing.

'OK. Let's move forwards a few more years. After successfully travelling back in time a few times, an attempt was made to travel forwards. Nobody thought that this would produce much of a problem, but they were all wrong. You see, the problem with travelling forwards is that none of it has happened yet. If you want to go back, it's like rewinding a video'. He smiled and congratulated himself for using the antiquated term. 'Yes, a video. The film is already there to see. But going forwards is another matter. It has to be mapped out. The future isn't there. The computer has to speculate what's going to happen'.

'The computer guesses the future?' asked Zak incredulously. This may seem like a silly question, but what if it gets it wrong?'

'That was the initial problem. The computers had terabytes - even exabytes of information about the world, about people, about life, about history. All stored in their data banks. It used all of this to predict a future, but unfortunately, the initial attempts got it very wrong. We suspect that it was only twenty-five percent right. The TTT who jumped forward was never seen again. As far as we could deduce, the future world that the computer created must have been completely different to the world that we are living in now. It was either a far better place, so wonderful that he didn't want to return. Or...'

Or he was killed by a futuristic computer virus' said Zak astounded.

'Yes. That's a good way of putting it' said Ron cheerfully. 'You have to remember that all TTT's were volunteers. The first trip to the future was almost as popular as my first trip to the past'.

'It's a shame that you weren't used again' said Julie.

'Oh, I couldn't' said Ron, missing the sarcasm in Julie's voice. 'It would hardly be fair to let me go again. I wasn't in the running for that particular race'.

'Anyway, we're drifting a bit here' said Ron waving his hand in a circular motion as if he was winding the story along. 'The problem was future travel. The computer couldn't cope. It took years of work before the breakthrough was finally made. It was six years later, in the year 2015 when the predicted future percentage started to rise. We've now got it up to eighty percent. And it was all down to a brilliant kid on the team. He joined the company in 2012 at the age of just seventeen.

'Seventeen? You're telling me that a seventeen-year-old boy worked out all the bugs connected to future time travel?' said Zak. This story was getting more and more amazing by the minute, but it finally had Zak hooked. Could anyone really make up something this bizarre?

'Oh, he was twenty when he cracked it. You know what kids are like with computers. He was using one at the age of four. By the time he left school he was a computer genius'.

'And you say he got the percentage up to eighty' said Julie. 'So, here's a question? If its only eighty percent right, then how are we here? How have we travelled into the future?'

'Ah, but you haven't' said Ron. 'We've picked you up from the past. This future is already written. We can only go forwards from "here" at an eighty percent accuracy'.

Julie's brain was hurting, trying to get her head around it all. 'It still sounds very risky. I mean, I certainly wouldn't be first in the queue to volunteer'.

Ron laughed. 'Don't worry my dear. I wouldn't dream of sending you'. He turned to Zak and a malicious grin spread across his face. 'Why would I bother when I can send Zak?'

Chapter 27 – "The Control Room"

Zak and Julie stared at him in disbelief.

'You must be out of your mind' said Julie.

'You crazy bastard' said Zak.

'You'll kill him' said Julie.

Ron laughed. 'Isn't it amazing how you can come around to an idea so quickly' he said. 'You didn't even believe in time travel five minutes ago. You seem convinced enough to be concerned about it now'.

Zak composed himself. 'You're right' he said. 'I don't believe it. What am I worrying for?'

'Then you won't mind volunteering' said Ron brightly.

'No' screamed Julie. 'You can't make him do this'. She turned to Zak. 'Think about it. The balloons, the robots. This stuff just doesn't exist. And how did we get here. This story, although absurd may have some truth in it'.

'But time travel?' said Zak. 'In the twentieth century?'

'Twenty first' Ron pointed out smugly. 'You keep forgetting'.

'And the crystal balls' continued Julie ignoring him. 'You saw the power. They must be the heart of this'.

'Clever girl' said Ron. 'I'd forgotten that you'd seen the crystal rooms. Cost us a fortune to replace the one that you broke'.

'The one that *we* broke ' said Zak turning on Ron angrily. 'It nearly killed us. We were only just saved by the door'.

'Yes. You've got me to thank for that' said Ron. 'I couldn't let my prize guinea pig be killed before I had a chance to use him. The doors to the crystal chambers are supposed to be kept closed when the time machine is in use. You stepped in at the wrong moment. Upset the equilibrium'.

'It was in use?' said Julie. 'You mean. Someone was travelling? And us being there caused the ball to explode?'

'Exactly. Didn't do the TTT much good either. He's still in the hospital wing recovering'.

Julie gasped 'What happened to him?'

'It was a bit nasty really. There are one hundred crystals you see. Each one is responsible for one percent of the operation. The machine effectively scans the TTT at a molecular level and breaks him, or her, into a hundred blocks of data. Each block contains over a million pieces of information that make up a section of the body. When the crystal exploded, one of the blocks was lost when he was put back together'. Ron shook his head dismayed.

'Oh my God' said Julie horrified. 'Which bit was missing?'

'The block that was lost contained all the data that made up his left hand. When he appeared, the hand didn't appear with him. He would have bled to death if we weren't quick enough'.

'Isn't there a system to check that all the blocks are present before he travels?' said Zak sickened.

'Yes, but unfortunately, the crystal blew after all the checks had been made. It was a very unlucky piece of timing. A fraction of a second either way and he would have been fine. We've got somebody working on it now. It won't happen again'.

'Doesn't this make you realise how dangerous this whole thing is?' said Julie, turning back to Zak. 'He could have easily been killed. What if something important had gone missing. I mean – something internal'.

'As I said, it won't happen again' said Ron. 'This is the first crystal we've lost. We don't normally have people running around the crystals when the machine is in use'.

There was a stunned silence which Ron finally broke. 'OK. Let's get back to the matter in hand. We propose to send you thirty years into the future' he said to Zak. 'About 2047. We will surgically implant a camera on the inside of your eye'.

Julie was about to protest, but Ron raised his hand to stop her.

'It's common procedure for TTT's now so you've got nothing to worry about. All you have to do is wander around for a couple of hours taking in the sights. We will record what you see and hear at all times'.

'Oh, and do try to stay inconspicuous' he added.

'Inconspicuous?' said Zak, his anger rising again. 'I'm from 1994. I'm going to look a little bit out of place fifty odd years in the future. How on Earth can I stay inconspicuous? What do you want me to do? Wear a hat?'

Ron laughed. 'People haven't changed much in the last thirty years. We have no reason to believe that they will change in the next thirty' he said. 'Fashions change, technology obviously changes', he waved his hand around the room. 'Even countries change. But people? People on the whole don't change a lot. You won't get in any danger just observing. After two hours, we will instruct the machine to bring you back'.

'No danger? Tell that to the last poor sod who went forward' said Zak. 'Oh, wait a minute, you can't because you never saw him again'.

'We made a mistake there' admitted Ron. The recall sequence was out of our hands. Only he had the power to bring himself back, and for some reason he decided to stay. We've improved things since then. It can be done either way now'.

'So, I can come back when I want to?'

'Actually – No. We're not going to give you that option. We don't want you to recall yourself after a few seconds. It costs too much, and we want to gather some useful data from your visit first'.

'Costs too much?' exploded Zak. 'Surely cost isn't the issue here. I'm not going without an emergency way out'.

Ron looked Zak in the eye. 'I'm afraid you don't have much choice' he said coldly. He pressed a button on his chair and the guards came in. 'Take this man to surgery'.

****

Zak awoke to find himself in a recovery bay. The surgery had only taken place a couple of hours ago and a painful ache emitted from his left eye. The last thing he remembered was being dragged away helplessly by the two burly guards. He had been given a strong sedative which had ebbed away his remaining strength before he had even left the room.

He looked around and was startled to see Julie sleeping on a similar bed opposite him. Oh no. Not her too, he thought. They can't send Julie. He swung his legs off the bed and found that they weren't working properly yet, and he had to drag himself across the floor to get to her bed. He hoisted himself up and managed to get his elbows onto it.

She was just stirring. He shook her gently and her eyes flickered open.

'What's the…..going on?' she mumbled. 'Zak?'

'Are you OK?' he said.

'Tired' she said sleepily.

Zak examined her eyes but couldn't see any sign of bruising or stitching. He ran his finger over his own eye and winced as he clearly felt the neat stitches running from left to right just above the eyebrow. He waited for a few minutes for Julie to wake up properly. After a while, he found the strength was returning to his legs and he managed a few tentative steps around the room.

'What happened?' he said when she was full awake.

'They dragged you away' she replied, sitting up carefully.

'To you, I mean? Why are you here?'

'I wasn't far behind. I tried to stop them and got a needle pushed into me as well. That's the last thing I remember'.

'So what now?' said Zak. 'If this time travel story is true, then I'm about to become the worlds first future time traveller'.

'You mean the second' said Julie grimly. 'Do you believe him now?'

'Well, I don't think they'd bother to operate on me if it's just a joke' said Zak. 'It's a bit extreme. How bad is my eye? I wish there was a mirror around here somewhere'. He tottered back to Julie's bed and she examined the eye.

'Oh God. You look hideous' she said horrified. 'Your eyebrow has an eyebrow. You look like the elephant man's slightly uglier brother'.

'So glad you can have a joke at my expense at a time like this' he said grumpily.

'It's fine' she laughed. 'It's been stitched up very well. You won't have much of a scar when it heals. Can you feel the camera?'

'Can't feel a thing' he said. 'Just a bit sore when I poke it. You wouldn't think there was anything there'.

'Perhaps there's not' she said hopefully. 'Perhaps it's all an elaborate hoax'.

'Maybe' he said.

Suddenly the door slid open and four guards stood before them.

'Or maybe not' said Julie miserably.

'Does this mean we've got to go? Said Zak sarcastically. 'I wanted a matching one in the other eye. So I can see in stereo'.

The guards said nothing but bustled Zak and Julie out of the room, Julie staggering most of the way, the strength not fully returned to her legs yet.

'Friendly bunch aren't they' said Zak. 'I wonder where Ron found them'.

'Probably hiding in a cave in the stone age' said Julie, which earnt her a particularly hard shove from the nearest thug.

They were escorted to a room that could only have been the control room that Zak had heard of earlier. There was hi-tech equipment everywhere. Switches, knobs, giant computer screens displaying digital maps and charts, and standing in the middle of the room, in all its glory, was the time machine.

At first glance, it was just a large glass dome. There was nothing inside it except a red cross painted on the floor, presumably where the TTT stood, thought Zak. It could probably hold four or five people maximum unless they really bunched up together. On closer inspection, Zak noticed that the red cross was actually made up of thousands of tiny LED's connected by cables beneath the dome. Cables that snaked for miles around the building like veins, joining the crystals with the computers and finally here to the heart of the system.

'Welcome to my hobby room' said Ron with pride. 'Isn't it something? This is what years of hard work and dedication can achieve. Years of blood sweat and tears. This is a dream come true'.

'More like a nightmare' said Julie quietly, looking around the room in awe. This had suddenly become very real. 'Where is everyone? I'm surprised that this place isn't overrun with operators and technicians. Experts?'.

'That's the beauty of the time machine' said Ron. 'A child could operate it. It's so simple. Let me give you a guided tour'.

He signalled the guards to leave the room and to Zak and Julie's amazement they were left alone with Ron.

You look surprised' said Ron. 'Just because my robots aren't here, I wouldn't get any ideas. He pointed to various cameras around the room. 'We monitor everything in here, and we have an extra camera now. Your eye is linked in too. Take a look at this'.

He indicated a large screen on the wall, touched the screen a few times, and an image appeared. As Zak moved his head, the picture changed. He swung his head to look at Julie, and her picture appeared clearly on the screen'.

'Another breakthrough in modern technology said Ron proudly. 'These cameras are being used by spies all over the world. They were developed by our company too. We wanted them to monitor the past, and now the future. You should be honoured that you are the chosen TTT'.

Ron turned his back on them and walked to another screen displaying a map of the world. Zak pounced. He knew that he was being watched. He knew that they would probably be on him within a matter of seconds, but if he could just land one good punch on Ron's nose it would be worth it.

He was two steps away when a stabbing pain hit him between the eyes and he fell to the ground blinded, clutching at his face.

'I did warn you' said Ron as Zak howled in pain. 'You're being watched all the time. Don't worry. It will only last about twenty seconds. It's a little extra we built into the camera. It just tweaks the nerve a bit. Temporarily blinds you.

Zak's vision suddenly returned to normal and the pain slowly subsided.

'Hurts like hell apparently' said Ron brightly.

'You bastard' said Zak rubbing his eyes.

'Hey. Watch the stitches. Do you want to go back to surgery? That was just a warning. I'm sure you won't try anything again. Now – Take a look at this'.

He stood in front of another screen that was covered in numbers. At the top of the screen were the words "Destination. Please select Date and Time".

'This is where we enter your destination' said Ron. 'We can choose any place, any time'.

He touched the on-screen keypad and tapped the 0, then 7 followed by 0,6,2,0,4,7,1,3,0,0. A message popped up

CONFIRM 7TH JUNE 2047 13:00?

Ron touched "Yes". A warning in red flashed up at the bottom of the screen.

DATE IS IN THE FUTURE. ARE YOU SURE?

Again, Ron pressed the "Yes" option. After a second the screen changed to a map of the world. He turned to Zak.

'Where would you like to go?' he said with a grin.

'You mean you can send me anywhere?' said Zak astounded, the pain in his eyes all but forgotten.

'Anywhere in the world. We've used it as a teleporting machine before. It can send a man to the opposite side of the world in a matter of seconds. It's a bit quicker than flying. Mind you, it costs quite a bit more too, so we only use it in emergencies'.

'How can that possibly work?' said Julie. 'Although it's difficult enough to believe in time travel, the thought of transferring him to a different country is just as impossible'.

'It's not as complicated as you think' said Ron. 'Scanning and breaking the TTT down into data is the hard bit. Once he's in the computer as ones and zeroes, he can be sent anywhere. We have our own satellites now. In the early days, we experimented with phones. Sending data down a phone line was common practice – even in your time'.

'How will it pinpoint where I'm going to?' said Zak. 'You can't have every place in the world stored in the computer'.

'Of course we have' said Ron. It's a very small part of the project and barely takes up any disk space or processing power. I'll show you'.

He touched the world map on Europe and the picture zoomed in closer. Then he touched England, and a map of England came into focus. Then London. Then Downing street.

'We have every address in the world mapped. We can search by postcode, or street, or even just zoom in to a field somewhere and select that as a destination'

'But how does it know where Downing Street is?' said Julie perplexed.

'All places are programmed with the correct latitude and longitude' said Ron. 'If I accept this as the destination, the computer will send Zak's data to the satellite, and the satellite will transmit it down at exactly the right point, in the correct sequence of course, so that he is put back together properly'.

'This is amazing' said Zak. 'If this actually works it will be the most astonishing machine ever built'.

'Of course it works' said Ron. 'How do you think we got you here?'

Zak thought for a moment. 'I don't know. Wouldn't you need a time machine at the other end to bring us back?'

'No. As I said, the TTT has his own means to come back. It's like a personal scanner and transmitter, but it will also scan anything he's holding on to. Bringing you back was easy. All we had to do was travel to you, knock you on the head, and then scan and beam you back while holding your hand. The machine does the rest. It took less than thirty seconds'.

'Hang on a minute' said Julie. 'Where do I fit into all of this? Or Zak for that matter. Why did we get chosen to come here?'

Ron grinned. 'I've not told you that part yet have I? I'll tell you when Zak comes back. It will give him something to look forward to'.

'If I come back you mean' said Zak. 'Anything could happen in the two hours that I'm gone'.

'You'll be fine' said Ron. 'Can't you trust me?'

'No' retorted Zak. 'If this machine can only generate a world that is eighty percent correct, then I can't help but to have a few trust issues right now'.

'Why can't you wait a bit longer?' said Julie. 'You've got the percentage up to eighty. Can't you wait until it hits one hundred?'

'There's a bit of a snag there' admitted Ron. 'You see – Marcus, this brilliant kid on the team I was telling you about. Well – He's the only one would knows how to do it. He raised the accuracy from twenty-five to eighty alone'.

'What happened to him' asked Julie.

'He revolted' said Ron embarrassed. 'Disappeared. He's travelling through different times, checking up on his past. Normally you have to return home before travelling again, but he built a device that allows him to access the computers directly. I did say he was a genius. He can jump from anywhere. We've sent TTT's looking for him. But he's always at an advantage'.

'Zak smiled. 'Isn't that a shame' he said sarcastically. 'Poor Ron can't get his machine to work properly because his prize pupil found a better way to live his life'.

'It doesn't bother me' said Ron dismissively. 'He'll come back one day – and we'll nab him then. It's you who should be worried. If it wasn't for Marcus running off, you would be facing better odds than eighty percent right now'.

'Anyway', he said. 'Time for business. I could talk to you all day, but I think it's time for you to leave'.

Chapter 28 – "Marcus"

Ron turned and cancelled the Downing Street destination.

'I think the prime minister might be a bit surprised if you showed up out of the blue' he said as his fingers flashed over the screen. 'I've already set your destination. I'm going to send you to France. The Eiffel tower to be precise. You won't look so much out of place if you can't speak the language. They'll just think you're a tourist, which technically – you are'.

He grabbed what looked like a watch and passed it to Zak.

'Put this on' he said. 'As soon as you arrive it will begin a two-hour countdown. When you have five minutes left, I want you to find somewhere out of the way to return back home. I don't want people to see you disappearing out of the blue'.

'Why not? They're bound to see me appear in such a crowded place'.

'Not true' said Ron. 'Another feature of the time machine is that it has an option to drop you in an area where there are no people. Remember, it has predicted this world, so knows exactly where everyone is in the drop zone. Of course, you could end up being several hundred yards from the tower, but at least you won't be seen'.

He touched the screen again, and a confirmation list appeared:-

DESTINATION:	EIFFEL TOWER, PARIS, FRANCE
LATITUDE:	48.8584° N
LONGITUDE:	2.2945° E
DESTINATION DATE:	07TH JUNE 2047
DESTINATION TIME:	13:30
RETURN TIME:	15:30
CLEAR DROP ZONE:	YES

PLEASE MAKE YOUR WAY TO THE DOME

Ron turned to Zak. 'I believe that last message is for you' he said. 'Are you going to go on your own accord, or do we have to do this the hard way?'

Zak remembered the excruciating pain in his eye that he had endured before and decided that he didn't want to suffer that again.

'Please' he said. 'Can you let me have the option to come back on my own? Anything could happen. I need an emergency way out. If this thing kills me, I'm not going to be able to give you any information about the future world. It will all be for nothing'.

Ron pondered the idea for a moment and then smiled. 'Sorry Zak. I can't do that. You've got nothing to worry about though. The picture from your camera will be monitored all the time. I promise that you'll be brought back if you're in any danger'.

'You can see what I see all the time I'm there?' said Zak amazed.

'We think so' said Ron. 'It's a fairly new gadget. Works pretty well when travelling back in time, but obviously it hasn't been tested this way. We're fairly optimistic though'.

'Fairly? Great – That fills me with confidence' said Zak sarcastically.

Ron laughed. 'Perhaps you'll learn to trust me when you get back' he said. 'You never know. We might even become friends'.

'Fat chance' said Zak under his breath as he walked towards the large dome in the middle of the floor.

'Wait' cried Julie, rushing up to him. She threw her arms around him and hugged him. 'Please don't send him' she begged Ron. 'What if he doesn't come back?'

'You're not helping him Julie' warned Ron. 'This is hard enough for him already. Let him go. He'll be back before you know it. Then I'll give you both the full story'.

Julie sobbed and Zak held her tight. 'I've got no choice' he said softly. 'Try not to worry'.

He kissed her and gently pushed her back towards Ron. He took a deep breath and entered the dome.

****

As the door to the dome slid shut, an overwhelming sense of dread came over Zak. He found he was also tingling with excitement though. However dangerous the next two hours were going to be, he couldn't help being a bit curious of what lay ahead.

He heard a whirr, that increased in volume as the machine powered up, and a static charge began to build. The familiar tugging came from the hairs on the back of his neck and his heart began to beat faster. He could just about hear Ron's voice outside.

'I think I'll let you do the honours my dear' he said. Julie's eyes were still red from crying, and now they opened wide in dread.

'I can't' she said, 'I can't send him. I won't. You'll have to do it'.

Ron move quickly, grabbed her angrily and dragged her over to the screen.

'Press it' he ordered. 'Press it or Zak gets another bolt between his eyes'.

Tears began to stream down her face again as her hand stretched towards the screen. She hesitated and turned away as she thumped the 'Send' option in despair. A clear pleasant voice rang out.

"Time circuits initiated. Countdown Commencing".

"10"

Julie stared across the room helplessly at Zak in the large glass dome.

"9"

Zak turned around to face Julie. The static had increased and the droning noise coming from the dome almost drowned out the countdown. He could just about hear it.

"8"

Ron stood patiently, no expression on his face. He truthfully didn't know what Zak was going to encounter in a future world that was generated with a twenty percent defect.

"7"

The one hundred crystal balls in the many rooms of the complex began their rhythmic pulsating through their many colours.

"6"

Julie tried to walk towards Zak, but Ron reached out and put a warning hand on her shoulder.

"5"

There was a blinding flash and suddenly Julie lost track of what was going on. A man appeared from thin air in the space between her and Zak, wielding a kind of gun that she had never seen before. Julie and Ron gaped in astonishment and a second passed before anyone reacted.

"4"

'Marcus' said Ron under his breath.

The door burst open and four guards rushed in brandishing guns.

"3"

'Stop the countdown' ordered Marcus. He turned towards the dome. 'Or I'll break the glass'.

'Don't be a fool Marcus' shouted Ron. 'You'll kill us all. Even a crack in the dome will cause it to explode'.

"2"

Marcus pulled the trigger and a laser appeared from the end of the gun blasting a hole in the far wall, inches from the side of the dome.

'You're bluffing. Stop the countdown' he shouted, training the gun on the glass this time. Zak was watching this unfold in front of him in amazement and he ducked for cover. He didn't know who this guy was, but he had a crazy look in his eyes that made him look like a madman – and he was pointing a gun straight at him.

"1"

Ron grabbed Julie around the throat and produced his own gun, holding it to her head.

'Put the gun down Marcus' he said viciously. 'I swear, I'll blow her brains all over the floor'.

'Nooooo' screamed Julie. 'But it was too late'.

"Scanning complete. Sending"

There was another blinding flash, this time from the dome and a surge of power filled the room. Zak felt as if his was being ripped into a hundred pieces. Every part of his body seemed to pull in a different direction than the piece next to it. The power from the red cross surged through him like a million volts. The hair on his head stood straight in the air, and a scream caught in his throat. It all took a fraction of a second.

The flash cleared and Julie rubbed her eyes in disbelief.

Zak was gone.

****

Marcus was the first to react. He swung the gun around and shot a laser at the guards. The blast caught two of them and they fell like stones. He was moving immediately and dived into a roll that took him to the far side of the dome away from the others.

'Give it up Marcus' yelled Ron, reaching behind him as he spoke. He had waited for the day that Marcus would return, and he had prepared for it. He flicked a switch on the panel behind him and the screen lit up a new message.

TIME CIRCUITS DISABLED

The two remaining guards stood at the other side of the dome making sure that Marcus couldn't get a clear shot at Ron.

'It's OK. Back off' said Ron calmly to the guards. 'Leave him alone. He's not going anywhere'

'Let her go Ron' said Marcus. 'You don't need her. You've got Zak. Let Julie go'.

Julie hadn't recovered yet from losing Zak. And was finding it difficult to breath because of Ron's vice like grip around her throat but was still surprised to see this stranger using their names.

'I can't do it Marcus' said Ron. 'Give yourself up now and I'll give you your job back. You could still prove useful to me'.

'I wouldn't work for you again at any price' said Marcus. 'Let her go'.

'You see, that's your problem Marcus' said Ron. 'You've got yourself into a no-win situation. You're going to *have* to work with me if you want to save Zak's life'.

'Where have you sent him you bastard?' said Marcus through gritted teeth.

Ron laughed. 'Surely you mean "When" have I sent him. Do you think you're capable of hitting that magical one hundred percent?' he said with a grin. 'I hope so for Zak's sake'.

Marcus visibly sagged. 'You couldn't have. You wouldn't do it Ron. Even you're not stupid enough to send someone forward again'.

'Sorry Marcus. I couldn't wait for you forever. I had to know. I had to know what was out there'.

'Then you've already killed him' said Marcus quietly 'He won't stand a chance'.

'He will if you cooperate' said Ron. 'You see. One thing we have on our side is time. If you can get that machine working one hundred percent, then I'll send you forward too - exactly one minute after him. You should be able to bring him back before anything nasty happens'.

Marcus considered his options. He only had one. He had to go back and rethink his strategy. He reached down to his belt to a small device about the size of a calculator with a selection of buttons on it.

'I'm afraid you're going to have wait a bit longer Ron' he said. 'Don't worry Julie. I'm going for Zak. I can fix this'.

He wanted to set her mind at ease before he left. He didn't have a clue what he was going to do though. He pressed a button on the calculator shaped device.

Nothing happened. He tried again.

'Not having a problem are you, dear boy?' said Ron cheerfully. 'You see, I always knew you'd return one day, so I built some software to jam the time circuits. You won't be travelling any time soon from here'.

'Shit' said Marcus under his breath. How could he have been so stupid, and let Ron get one over on him.

'Drop the gun and come and meet Julie' said Ron. 'I'm sure you've been dying to make her acquaintance for years'.

Marcus put the gun in his belt and stepped out from behind the dome, walking slowly towards Ron with his hands stretched out beside him. He had blown it.

'Not good enough Marcus. Drop it' ordered Ron.

Marcus plucked the gun from his belt and tossed it on the floor. Ron loosened his grip from Julie's throat and pushed her away as she gasped a lungful of fresh air.

Marcus went to her. 'Are you OK?' he said, examining the bruises around her throat.

'Just about' she gasped. 'Who are you? How do you know me?'

Ron laughed at Marcus' look of astonishment.

'You mean you haven't told them yet?' he said flabbergasted.

'I promised them the full story when Zak gets back' said Ron. 'I'll let you have the honours if you like. You can tell them both together'.

'He won't be coming back' said Marcus sadly. 'Not unaided. Let me go after him now. I'll fix the machine for you when I've bought him safely back. I've been working on it while I've been away, and I think I've cracked it'.

'You'll fix the machine first' said Ron impatiently. 'If I open up the time circuits you could go anywhere. Zak can wait. Even if it takes you months to fix. I can send you forwards immediately after him. You can still bring him back safely'.

Marcus knew he couldn't win. 'OK. But let me talk to Julie first. It isn't fair to leave her waiting. Give me an hour?'

Ron looked at his watch. 'You know what? Why not. I've not had a chance to eat yet this morning. You have an hour, then I want you working on that machine'.

He turned to the guards. 'Take these two downstairs'.

Chapter 29 – "Surprises"

'I hope you can take another surprise' said Marcus when they were finally alone. 'I'm sure you've had enough for one day'.

'I don't think I can be surprised any more' she said. 'Is Zak going to be OK?'

'Maybe. I'm not going to lie. I don't think he's going to come back on his own accord. I've no idea what kind of future he's in at the moment'.

'Can you fix the machine?' said Julie. 'Can you get it working properly. To one hundred percent I mean. You said you'd cracked it'.

Marcus looked away embarrassed. 'No' he said sadly. 'I think it's impossible. I *have* been working on it ever since I left, but I can probably only get it up to about eighty-eight, but the rest….' he shrugged his shoulders. 'Who knows? Not anytime soon'.

'We still stand a chance though' he added. 'Ron doesn't know much about it. I think I could bluff him into thinking that I've fixed it. I've been away for a long time'.

'I suppose it's worth a try' said Julie doubtfully. 'Is he likely to fall for it?'

'Probably not. There is one more thing that might work though. If we can get the time circuits switched back on, we can use this'. He showed her the device that was strapped around his waist.

'You can travel using that?'

'Yes. I set up a secure sub-program on the computer before I left. It allows me to connect to the main server from anywhere, and it's blocked from Ron. He can't disable it completely. It will start working again when he switches the time circuits back on'.

'I'm surprised he hasn't taken it away from you already. He's not going to let you keep it for long' said Julie.

'I know. That's why I want you to have it'. He slipped it off and gave it to Julie.

'Me? What can I do with it' said Julie looking horrified.

'Ron has to switch back on in two hours so he can bring Zak back' said Marcus. 'If he can bring him back' he added solemnly. 'He'll never suspect that you've got this. If he doesn't figure it out, then you can jump forward and get Zak back'.

'You must be joking' Anything could happen to me'.

'That's a risk that one of us has got to take if we want to save Zak. Ron will expect me to try something. It makes more sense to try and send you'.

Julie protested again, but Marcus was insistent.

'All you have to do is go in, grab Zak, and then return again. You could probably do it in less than ten seconds'.

'Do you know if the time machine can even bring someone back from the future? I mean, it's never been done before has it?'

He ignored the question. 'You'll be fine' he said. 'Here. Strap it around your waist underneath your clothes'.

Julie did as she was told but she wasn't happy about it.

'I'm going to need the longitude and latitude so that you can travel to exactly the same place' said Marcus, thinking aloud. 'I can get that from the computer later. After that, all you have to do is press this button'. He pointed to a red button on one side. 'And to return, you press this one'. A green one. 'If you can't find Zak, you can always come back on your own'.

Julie wasn't really taking this in. Who was this guy? Could she trust him? He could be working with Ron and this could part of a bigger plan. She looked him in the eye.

'How do I know I can trust you?' she said. 'I mean, where do you fit into all of this? How do you know about me and Zak?'

'OK. Here goes' said Marcus. 'I did promise another surprise, didn't I?'. He sat and pondered for a second. 'It's difficult to know where to begin. Ron's really screwed things up by bringing you two here. You see. That never happened first time around'.

'What do you mean "first time around"?'

'I want you to assume you are back in 1994. Remember that the time machine wasn't invented until much later. You and Zak got married in early 1995…..'.

'Hang on. I never met Zak until I came here'.

'No. You were brought here in March. You wouldn't have met Zak until later in the year. You were married very quickly. That part of your life probably won't happen the same now…because of Ron, but it's important to the story'.

'OK. I think' said Julie slowly.

'Right. In 1995, you had a baby'. Julie's eyes opened wide.

'A baby? You must be joking'.

'That's only part of the surprise. You see, that baby was me'.

Julie's brain began to hurt. 'You're my son?' she said sarcastically. 'But you're only a few years younger than me'.

'You have to remember that you're in the future now. I was born in 1995. It's 2017 now. I'm twenty-two years old.

Julie thought about it. It was possible. He even looked a bit like Zak. She hadn't really noticed until now.

'I'm sorry to land it on you like this' said Marcus. 'It's a lot to take in I know. But you have to know the whole story'.

'My son' said Julie amazed. She couldn't believe what she was being told. A week ago, she was just a single girl who was struggling to find a relationship. Suddenly she had a husband and a twenty-two-year-old son. 'Carry on' she gasped sinking into her chair. 'What else can you tell me about myself?'

You probably won't like the next bit' said Marcus. 'But it kind of fills in some of the holes. Just before you met Zak, you were going out with another man. You hadn't been together for long, but it looked like it was going places. If Zak hadn't appeared on the scene, who knows. You may have married him instead. It wasn't to be though. Zak came along and you fell head over heels in love with him. The other guy didn't stand a chance'.

Another man? Julie had been single for so long and now she had two men fighting for her affections. She was struggling to get her head around this new piece of news, that she nearly missed what Marcus said next.

'The other man was Ron. You have to remember that he was about the same age as you then. He was probably quite a catch in his more youthful days'.

'No way. That's not possible' said Julie defiantly. 'How could I have ever seen anything in Ron?'

Marcus shrugged. 'I'm sorry. It happened. The good news is - you left him for Zak. As you can imagine he was very bitter. He eventually met and married someone else, but he's carried around a hatred for Zak for many years'.

Julie was stunned. She wasn't sure if she wanted to hear any more.

'Anyway. It's 1995. You and Zak are happy, complete with baby - me, and from a very early age I had a fascination with computers. I was programming before I was ten, and by the time I left school I could've picked up a job anywhere. I worked a couple of jobs that bored me as there was no challenge, and eventually found T-Time - that's the company that owns this place. Ron had worked his way up to a very high level in the company and he became my mentor. When I joined, I was told all about the time travel project, and like you I was amazed. Here at last I had something that would really challenge me, and I was excited about working for the first time in my life'.

He paused to glance at his watch knowing that they didn't have long.

'They set me to work on the future-travel problem and it wasn't long before I started getting results' he continued. 'After a while I got bored though. I wanted to travel. They'd let me go back once, and I loved it and wanted to do more. They promised me six months off if I solved the future travel problem, but I was struggling and got impatient. So, I built the device you're wearing. While I was working for Ron, I was logged into the mainframe all the time, so it was easy to insert my own program and hide it. They had no idea and couldn't stop me'.

'I began to travel. It was like a dream for me. I liked to go back and watch you and Zak when you were younger. I always kept my distance though - I couldn't risk meeting you back then. There can be repercussions if you change anything. It's one of the golden rules of time travel'.

'After a couple of months, they caught me. I made the mistake of coming back here to get some stuff. I forgot to use the "Clear Drop Zone" function before travelling and appeared right in front of Ron. Frightened the life out of him' he laughed. 'At this point, I had two choices. I could stay and face the music, or I could travel again and continue with my life of travelling. It was probably a bit cowardly, but I chose the latter. Ron was marching me up to his office to tear strips off me when I disappeared. I've not seen his again since today'.

'Where did you go?' said Julie.

'I went everywhere' said Marcus. 'I don't normally stay in the same place for too long. It isn't much of a life, constantly being on the move, and as I said before, I get bored easily. After a while, I set myself the task of solving the future travel issue again but couldn't get past eighty-eight percent. If I'd reached one hundred, I would have had a whole new world of places to visit'.

'Of course, I kept going back to see you in the nineties. I couldn't return to my own time as Ron had told everyone that I'd had an accident at work and been killed. He had to cover up my disappearance without leaking the project out.

Marcus stretched and checked the time again.

'Anyway, one day, I went back to see Zak in 1994 – It was just before you had met. I waited and waited in my normal place, but he didn't show up. That was the only day that I risked meeting one of you. I went right up to the house and knocked on his door, but he wasn't there. I'd made the same trip before, and seen him, so I was bit surprised that he wasn't there. I tried jumping forwards a day at a time, then a week and then a month – but Zak had completely disappeared. Then I discovered that you had too. I finally found a newspaper claiming that you had disappeared without trace and were feared dead. In a different paper, it was claimed that Zak had escaped from a jail cell and was on the run.

'Prison?' said Julie startled. 'When was Zak ever in prison?'

'That's what I wanted to find out' said Marcus. 'I jumped back and forth for weeks trying to find out where he was last seen and what caused him to be sent to jail. To cut a long story short, he was found in the wrong place at the wrong time and was accused of murder. I nearly went back and prevented the murder, but I didn't want to meddle with the past. Instead, I just watched to see who really did it'.

'And who was it?' said Julie. She was completely intrigued with this story now, however mindboggling.

'His name was Bob Reshetna' said Marcus. 'He was a TTT. They broke their own rules'.

'They sent someone back to commit murder?' said Julie shocked. 'So they changed events in the future?'

'I think that was the idea. The guy they bumped off was a man called Don Connor. He was completely harmless, ran a video shop. I haven't proved it, but I believe he found out about T-Time and what they were working on, and spilt the beans. They went back and killed him to keep the project secret'.

'It didn't take long after that to figure out that you two had been abducted. It's Ron's dream to travel forward in time, you see. He isn't happy going backwards only. He wants to see what his future holds. If Zak had gone to jail, he would never have met you and I would never have come along. Ron believes that I can fix the machine to work for future travel. Nobody else got even close to the results that I did'.

'So, he had to make sure that me and Zak got together?'

'Exactly. Can you imagine how that made him feel? He hated Zak and loved you but had to get you guys together to ensure that he had me working on the project. It must've killed him'.

'So, he brought us here, tormented us and put us through hell so that when we met, we'd lean on each for support?' said Julie thinking about it. 'And, it worked perfectly'.

'One thing you can say about Ron' said Marcus. 'He's a clever guy. To be fair, you two always had a spark. He just gave you both a little push'.

'But how come you're still here?' said Julie puzzled. 'I haven't had a baby now that I've been brought here'.

'I can only guess part of it' said Marcus. 'Ron wouldn't send Zak to the future and put him in danger unless…'

'Unless I'm already pregnant' said Julie with a gasp holding her belly. 'That's what Ron meant when he said the experiment was complete'.

'Right. I'd imagine that some time in the future, after I've been born, Ron will send the baby back and put me in the adoption system or something. I'd be raised by different parents'.

'Something doesn't make sense' said Julie. Actually, a lot of it didn't make sense in her mind right now. 'If that was the case, then you wouldn't have any memories of us now'.

'Right now, I'm still the Marcus that was your son first time around. You're carrying a Marcus that is likely to have a different past to mine. Different parents, different childhood. Well, it depends how things turn out, I guess'.

Julie thought about this. 'But what about Zak? He isn't fundamental at this point? You can still exist without him? As far as Ron is concerned, Zak can die, and it won't matter in the slightest?'

'Precisely. The fact that I'm still here is a good sign for you though. Ron *has* to protect you. Well, at least for the next nine months'.

Julie ran her hands through her hair. It was so much to take in in one go. She thought she was doing quite well considering.

'So, our aim is to get Zak back and then return to our own time, get married and raise you?' she said. 'But what will you do? This isn't much of a life for you'.

'I will destroy the time machine' said Marcus. 'I haven't got a clue what the knock-on effect will be, but I know that it should never have been invented'.

'But won't everything happen again? The time machine will still be invented. This guy, Don will still be killed. Zak will be framed for his murder. Won't it all just turn full circle?'

'No. Zak was only framed for the murder because he was there. If we can pull it off, then he will know better next time. The time machine may still get invented, but your lives won't be affected by it'.

'It could get very confusing' said Julie.

'Ila. It already is - Mum' laughed Marcus.

'OK. Now that's really weird' she laughed. 'What if...'

She was interrupted by the door being opened.

'Looks like it's time to go' said Marcus. He helped Julie up and patted the bulge on her belly to remind her of the device that was strapped there. She had almost forgotten about it. Walking past the guards, she felt like a drug smuggler going through customs at the airport.

Chapter 30 – "100%"

Julie and Marcus were led to a large computer room. It brought back a lot of old memories for Marcus, but this was the first time Julie had seen it. Marcus sat at the computer terminal and punched in his old logon code.

'Just like old times' he said.

Julie strolled around in awe looking at the vast array of equipment around her.

'Is all of this necessary for the time machine?' she said.

'That's only a small part of it' said Marcus as his fingers thundered away on the keyboard. 'There are three more rooms as big as this. Then there's the hundred crystal rooms, and the control room. You have to remember the complexity of this project is enormous. There's so much processing power going on the background'.

'It's certainly impressive' said Julie walking over to where he sat. 'For all the wrong reasons though'.

Ron sauntered in and smiled when he saw Marcus working at the keyboard.

'Good to have you back on the team Marcus' he said. 'You should never have left. You were getting so close'.

'You may live to see your dream come true yet' said Marcus without turning around. On the keyboard he typed

`NOT A HOPE YOU MISERABLE BASTARD`

Julie stifled a giggle as he deleted it with a flourish.

'I hope your conversation was enlightening Julie' said Ron. 'I trust you're happy and understand why I had to bring you and Zak here now'.

'I'll be happy when I see Zak safely back' said Julie grimly. 'How long has he been gone now?'

'Just over an hour my dear. See, doesn't time fly. He'll be back before you know it'.

Marcus continued to type, doing his best to ignore Ron. He was already inserting some code that would bring the percentage up to eighty-eight. He had done the groundwork for this while he had been away, so the programs only needed tweaking. He was stuck now though. He didn't believe it was possible to make it any higher. As he typed, he thought about Julie. He wasn't happy about sending her after Zak. She was his mother after all. If only he could think of another way.

The idea hit him like a thunderbolt, and he stopped typing for a second. Why didn't he think of it before? It was too easy. He could switch the time circuits back on from here. All he had to do was find the program that Ron had installed and reverse it. Ron had probably buried it deep and secured it, but Marcus had left some backdoor security in the system that no one knew about. He should be able to bypass anything Ron had added. He glanced around, aware that Ron was only a few feet away. He needed to get him away from the terminal so Ron couldn't see what he was doing. He heard Julie speak.

'Have you been watching him? On the monitors I mean. Can we see where Zak is right now?'

Ron laughed. 'I'm afraid not' he said. 'I must confess that I told a little white lie back there. I thought it best to set Zak's mind at rest'.

'But the camera...?'

'Doesn't work through time' said Ron. 'Oh, it records while he's away, but we can't get the signal back. I can look at the footage later. I have a team of people working on the live link, but it's still in development. Could be years before they get it working'.

Julie looked at him in shock. 'You've got to bring him back' she demanded. 'Anything could be happening to him'.

'He'll be fine' said Ron nonchalantly. 'Won't he Marcus?'.

Marcus continued to type, more aware of Ron's presence now. Julie turned to him for confirmation and his fingers flew over the keyboard.

GET RON AWAY. HAVE IDEA.

'He'll be OK if I can get this damn machine working' he said.

'See. Nothing to worry about' said Ron happily. 'Marcus will have the machine working in no time'.

Marcus was already deleting the message, but Julie had seen it.

'Tell me what all of this is used for?' she said, walking towards the far end of the computer room. 'Is it all really necessary?'

Marcus held his breath and let it out in relief when Ron followed her up the room.

'This is just part of it my dear' he said. 'We have three rooms similar to this, bigger too....'.

Marcus grinned to himself. Julie had said exactly the right thing. Ron loved to boast about the technology. He rarely got the chance to impress someone. He returned to his work and tried another password – 2126122020. Ron always used numeric passwords that meant something to him. It was a secure way to have a complex password. Unknown to him, Marcus had worked this out, so he knew most of his passwords too.

'Shit. He's changed it' he mumbled to himself. He tried another - 421281310. Still no good. A bead of sweat trickled down his face and he wiped it away absent-mindedly. He tried a third - 122221320. Looks like Ron's been changing them, he thought. His backdoor password had got him so far, but he needed to crack this one more level of security. After a fourth attempt, he began to panic. He glanced around and saw that Julie and Ron were still down the far end of the room. He turned back and tried again.

A menu screen burst into life as the logon was accepted. His eyes lit up. Very careless Ron, he thought. You've not changed them all. He saw a new option on the screen at the bottom of the menu.

Time Circuit Control

He selected this and was presented with a time display and various options. It seemed that the circuits could only be switched on and off at a certain time from this level. He looked at his watch and set the circuits to be enabled in five minutes. He needed to get his device back from Julie and wasn't' sure if Ron would be alerted if he turned the circuits on immediately.

He checked on Ron and noticed that he was still a long way off. He quickly selected the "Journey Log" which listed previous trips and destinations. The screen filled with information and he whistled to himself. The time machine was being used an awful lot. He glanced down at the names and times. The most recent entry was Zak. His name wasn't there, but the year and place were.

20th June 2047, Eiffel Tower, Paris, France
Lat: 48.8584° N, Long: 2.2945° E

Why France? he thought. Most of the travelling used to be done within England, especially the experimental trips. Why would he send Zak to France? He didn't have time to think about it. He heard Ron's voice and it sounded much nearer. He glanced up again and saw them walking briskly towards him.

'Let me show you this' he heard Ron say as they approached.

Marcus turned back and quickly memorised the latitude and longitude for the Eiffel tower. He lunged for the "Exit" key, but his hand fell short as he spotted something on the screen. He stared in amazement for a few brief seconds, too stunned to do anything else.

Ron rushed past him without looking. 'Come on Marcus. I can't hear much tippy tapping on those keys. Get on with it'

Marcus visibly jumped and finally hit the "Exit" key. Did Ron see? He couldn't have. He was still moving towards the other side of the room. His heart was hammering as Julie walked past and saw an odd look on his face. She frowned and he gave her a brief smile and quickly typed

NEED DEVICE BACK

Julie nodded and hurried past after Ron, hardly breaking stride, and firing another meaningless question at Ron. Marcus sat back in his chair, his heart slowly returning to normal. His thoughts turned back to what he had seen on the screen. Did he imagine it? Was it possible?

There was an entry just below Zak's. A TTT had travelled yesterday. Forwards. To the Eiffel Tower on the 20th June 2047.

****

Marcus had two more things he needed to do while he was logged into the secure area. He had to prevent Ron from locking out the time circuits again. And, more importantly, he had to remotely connect to his device and set the destination. As he typed his mind was reeling.

Why did he send someone else forward?

Did they come back?

Is Zak going after him?

Can't be.

Why did he bother with Zak if someone was already jumping forward?

He drew a blank. He couldn't believe that Ron had sent somebody else forward. He knew the dangers until the machine was operating properly. It would be a suicide mission for a TTT. Unless….

Unless they had fixed it somehow. If that was true, then sending Zak still didn't make sense. He put it to the back of his mind while he overrode Ron's Time Circuit program. He set a new password so that Ron couldn't log back in reverse what he'd done.

He glanced at his watch. He had less than two minutes before the circuits came on again. He had to get that device back.

His fingers quickly flashed over the keyboard again as he accessed his own programs and found the one that allowed him to connect to his personal time travel device. He set the longitude and latitude and logged out of the secure area, and back to the work that Ron had set him to do. The percentage for the future time-travel read eighty-eight. Time for a bluff. He changed the program so that the number read one hundred. It might give him the distraction he needed.

He let out a whoop. 'Shit. I've done it' he yelled standing up and pushing his chair back. Ron and Julie dashed over and Ron stood over the computer screen looking as the figure in front of him.

'No way. That's impossible' he said staring at the screen. 'We've had people working on that since you left. You can't have done it that quickly'.

Marcus stood behind Ron, shielding Julie from him while she slipped the time device from her waist.

'I told you I'd been working on it while I was away' he said, as Julie put the device in the hand he held out behind him. 'It was just a matter of implementing my program and making a few tweaks'. He slipped the device on and pulled his shirt over it. It made a bit of a bulge, but he didn't have long to wait.

'You're bluffing Marcus' said Ron grimly 'I know how good you are, but there's no way you've done it already. You're not going after Zak without proof that this is right'.

Marcus laughed exasperated. 'What proof can I give you? Surely, my willingness to jump forwards is proof enough that I trust what I've done'.

'I'll send Julie' said Ron. 'But not after Zak. I'll send her even further forward'. Julie's eyes widened in horror.

'Why not?' said Marcus, sticking with his bluff. A few more seconds is all he needed. He stepped back behind Julie. 'I have no doubt that it will work'.

'I think I'll take this first' said Ron, reaching for Julie's waist. He had seen the bulge when he gave her the tour of the room and knew exactly what it was.

'Get your hands off me' said Julie pushing herself away from Ron and slapping his hands away. She retreated behind Marcus whose face had dropped. Ron had spotted that they had switched it back.

'Give me the device Marcus. You can't go anywhere with it'.

Marcus sagged and unbuckled the device from his waist. Julie stared at him in shock and he shot her a warning glance. He handed it over to Ron who took it smiling.

A guard burst into the room. 'Did you turn the time circuits back on Sir?'

'Of course not' said Ron impatiently. 'They're locked off until Zak is due back'.

'But they're not' said the guard. 'They came back on about a minute ago'.

Ron's face dropped and Marcus took his moment and leapt forward. He grabbed Ron by the throat and reached down to the device.

'Time for you to realise your dream Ron' he said, and pushed the button. There was a brilliant flash.

Ron disappeared.

Marcus disappeared too.

Chapter 31 – "Paris"

Zak seemed to lose all of his senses at once. He felt like he didn't exist. The feeling only lasted a fraction of a second, but it felt like an eternity. His vision came back first, shortly followed by the rest. He collapsed to the floor in a heap, dazed but aware of what had just happened. It had worked. It had actually worked. But what kind of world was he in?

He was within the shadow of the Eiffel tower, near a large grassy area under some trees. Paris was somewhere he'd never been before, but he guessed he was in a park. Everything appeared to be perfectly normal. If the computer had gone twenty percent wrong, it wasn't obvious what it was.

He stood up and headed across the grass towards the tower. As he walked, he felt that something wasn't quite right, and realised a second later that it was the air. The air was much cleaner, much fresher than usual. He felt relaxed as it cleaned through his system, flushing out the old, stale dirty air that he had always inhaled. Was this something to do with the error in the computer, or had they managed to get on top of the pollution problems that most major cities had in the twentieth century? He was just pondering this when he saw a light coming towards him.

He stood mesmerised watching as the light approached. It reminded him of the bird that Ron had set on him a couple of days ago. Was that all it was? Two days? So much had happened since then that it seemed like weeks. The light was picking up speed and coming straight at Zak. Suddenly it accelerated at an impossible rate and flew over Zak's head, so close that the rush of air it made knocked him back to the ground. He didn't have time to duck. He saw it disappear in the distance.

What was that? A plane? A car? There was no sound. Who knew what could move like that in 2047.

He picked himself up again, just in time to see a bright flash over to his left. The flash looked familiar. It was exactly the same as the one that he had seen in the control room before he had vanished. He remembered the man who had appeared out of nowhere and held a gun up to him. If this was the same man, then he could be dangerous. He watched as two men appeared in the same fashion that he had. They seemed to be struggling. One of them lashed out at the other, sending him flying. He heard a voice.

'Zak. Where are you?'

He ducked behind a clump of bushes and peered out at the man. He didn't trust anyone. The man turned in a circle and chose a direction at random, which happened to be the opposite way from Zak. Zak scurried up towards where the other man lay on the floor, keeping low so that he wouldn't be spotted.

He recognised him immediately. Ron. What was Ron doing here?

Ron was bleeding from the nose where the other guy had punched him and was trying to find his feet. It suddenly occurred to Zak that the guy walking away must be there to help him.

'Hey, I've over here', he shouted and waved at Marcus, who stopped in his tracks and turned around.

Marcus hurried back. 'Zak? Are you OK?'.

'I'm fine. What's going on? Where's Julie? Who are you?'

'No time to explain. Let's go?'. He grabbed Zak's hand and was about to punch a button on his device when Ron leapt at him with a roar.

Marcus fell to the ground hard and Ron was on top of him instantly, grappling for the device around his waist. He had Marcus pinned, and had a hand stretching towards the button when Zak hit him. Zak had looked forward to this moment since before they had met, and he made sure it counted. Ron tumbled over Marcus and fell onto the ground beside him. Zak didn't stop there, and kicked him once, twice in his kidneys, making him yell in pain.

Marcus jumped up again and grabbed Zak for a second time.

'No wait. Don't leave me here' screamed Ron, struggling to find his feet again, but not quite managing it.

'Have a good life Ron' said Zak.

Marcus punched the button and they disappeared.

****

Julie stared in disbelief. First, she'd lost Zak. Now Marcus had vanished too. What was she supposed to do now? She looked at the guard who was experiencing a similar dilemma. His boss had just disappeared, and he wasn't sure what his next actions should be either.

'Um. Don't move' he said, lifting the gun.

'I wasn't intending to' said Julie. 'Put the gun down. It's a bit unnerving. I can't exactly go anywhere can I?'

The guard hesitated, thought abut this for a moment and lowered the gun. 'Where did they go?' he said, still not sure what to do next.

'How the hell am I supposed to know?' said Julie running a hand through her hair in despair. 'I'm as surprised as you are'.

He walked slowly across the room, crossing to the spot where Ron and Marcus had been standing before they had vanished. Julie watched him closely, eyeing the gun.

'They travelled' said the guard, stating the obvious. 'Where did they travel to?'

'Like I said. How would I know?' said Julie exasperated. She assumed that Marcus had gone for Zak, and Ron had accidentally gone along for the ride, but she didn't want to tell this goon anything.

The guard's confused looked turned to dismay. 'He's gone after Zak. That's not what Ron planned'. He raised the gun again and pointed it back at Julie. 'Stay here'. He hurried towards the door, stopped and thought about it, and turned back. 'No. Come with me'. He walked back towards Julie and grabbed her arm.

'Hey. OK. I can walk on my own accord' she said shaking him off and heading for the door.

There was a blinding flash and Marcus and Zak appeared in front of them.

'Zak' cried Julie, throwing her arms around him. 'I thought I'd lost you'.

'Don't move' said the guard holding the gun up again and pointing it as Marcus.

'Drop the gun' said Marcus. 'You won't get Ron back if you shoot me'.

The guard thought about this and swung the gun round towards Zak and Julie.

'Where is he?' he said to Zak.

'In a safe place' said Zak with a grin. 'Would you like to go there too? I'm sure we can sort you out a visit'.

The guard looked puzzled for a second. He hadn't had to deal with a situation like this before. He was used to following orders, and he certainly hadn't actually had to shoot anyone before.

'Turn around' he said. 'Up against the wall'.

Marcus and Zak obliged, but Julie stood her ground. 'You won't shoot me' she said, stepping towards him. 'Put the gun down and I won't hurt you'. She had noticed that the guard couldn't cope with the situation. He seemed flustered, and now that she had stood up to him, he was even more nervous. He glanced anxiously over his shoulder looking for help and found no one there.

'Turn around' he said again, trying to make it sound more forceful, but not succeeding.

Julie was now right in front of him, the gun almost pressing into her chest. She kicked him as hard as she could between his legs. It was the last thing he was expecting, and he fell to his knees with a shriek, dropping the gun at her feet.

'Thank you' she said, picking the gun up and handing it to a startled Zak. 'Sorry about that. I did warn you though. The pain should subside in an hour or so'.

'Are you mad?' spluttered Marcus. 'He could have killed you'.

'I doubt it' she said. 'Anyway, I figured that you could have just gone back a minute and saved me if he did'.

'But I would have disappeared too' said Marcus, grabbing the gun off her. 'Along with this'. He pointed to the device on his belt 'I wouldn't have existed remember'.

Julie stared at him as this sunk in and she felt the strength in her legs disappearing. Zak only just stopped her from falling to the ground.

'Can someone tell me what the hell is going on?' he said.

Chapter 32 – "Randy"

Ron lay on the ground, battered and bleeding. Where did he go wrong? This should have been his dream, but it had turned into the worst nightmare possible. He was stuck in a future that wasn't built properly and he had no way to get back home.

Or did he? He sat upright suddenly, his mind focusing on the day before. Of course. Randy.

Randy had been a pain in Ron's arse for as long as he could remember. They weren't related – Ron just wasn't ready to tell Zak the real story about the boy, and the suggestion to Zak that Randy was his son served well in helping him screw with Zak's head even more.

Both Randy and Ruby were Zak and Julie's children. They hadn't intended to have more children after Marcus - Randy had been an accident, and a few years after that, Julie had started pining for a little girl, so along came Ruby.

Ron had kidnapped them just after Marcus had revolted and disappeared from T-Time. He was angry with Marcus for running off, and still had a hatred for Zak for stealing Julie from him, but more importantly, he needed someone to finish the time machine problems. His desperation meant that he would try anything.

He had been persuasive and friendly and convinced them that their mum had died, and that he was a distant relative who had promised to raise them. He had hoped that one of them might have the same genius and interest in computers that Marcus had had. If he could train them, they might be able to finish what Marcus had started. Ruby had turned out to be a lost cause, but Randy was a bright lad and was keen to learn. The boy was never shown any part of the time machine – that would come later, but he started to excel in computer theory and programming, just as his older brother had.

Eventually, he had got bored though and started to skip classes and run away. He was getting older, and had no friends, and had started asking questions, finally taking his sister and running away from the complex, hiding in the abandoned church. At the time, Ron was busy making his plans for Zak and Julie, so left them alone, figuring that they'd come back when they got hungry, and knowing that they couldn't escape. He grabbed the boy back later when they had all turned up at the complex and locked him up, fearing he would jeopardize Zak and Julie's blossoming relationship. He was just glad that the boy hadn't recognised the younger version of his parents.

Randy escaped again, through a vent in his room, much like his parents had been doing at the same time. He navigated through the ventilation system found himself peering down through the vent of the control room, just as a TTT was being sent. He was astonished when the man disappeared in front of his eyes, and nearly gave himself away as he gasped in shock. He sat watching the activity below for a couple of hours, listening to conversations, and piecing together what was going on. Ron was there a while, looking at maps, making a final decision where to send Zak. He watched Ron set the Paris destination, ready for Zak's trip the next day, and finally Randy was left alone. The boy lowered himself carefully down into the control room and started exploring.

Ron had returned just as Randy disappeared in a flash. The boy's inquisitive mind sent him thirty years into the future, without understanding any of the dangers. In a way, Ron wasn't too concerned. Randy was turning out to be nothing but trouble, and after Ruby's accident, the boy would be even more difficult. He was glad to be shot of him.

Lying battered, bleeding and with all hope lost, Ron realised he was even more glad now. Randy hadn't returned which meant that he was still here. If Randy was still here, then Ron had a way to get back home.

Chapter 33 – "Ron"

Julie was all over Zak again. 'Are you alright? What happened? Did it really work?'

'Hey. What's all the fuss about? I was only gone about two minutes' said Zak startled.

'Two minutes for you. It was over an hour for us' said Marcus. 'I travelled to a point just one minute after you. If I'd have left it too long, you would have probably died'.

'It seemed perfectly normal' said Zak, taking this in. 'I thought the computer was going to put me in an alien world, but I couldn't see anything wrong'.

'The air was bad' said Marcus. 'I noticed it as soon as I arrived. It wasn't normal. Couldn't you feel your lungs beginning to burn?'.

'But it seemed cleaner' said Zak. 'I assumed that the computer had developed an atmosphere that was better than our own'.

'I think it was one of many mistakes that the computer made' said Marcus. 'As you said, we were only there for a couple of minutes. It would be interesting to go back in an hour and see if Ron's still alive'.

'You left him there?' said Julie incredulously. 'How will he get back?'

'He won't' said Marcus flatly. 'His dream was to see the future. At least he got what he wanted'.

'And what he deserves' said Zak with a grin. He turned to Marcus 'Are you going to tell me what I've missed? And who you are? Last time I saw you, you were pointing a gun at me'.

Marcus laughed. 'I'll give you the short version' he said. 'We've got work to do. I want to get you reinstated back in 1994. It's just as important for me as it is for you.

****

Twenty minutes later, they carefully made their way towards the control room, Zak in the lead brandishing the guard's gun.

'I can't take all of this in?' he said shocked. 'Julie and me married? You're my son? Is this some kind of a joke?'

'I'm afraid not' laughed Julie. 'I'm still trying to process it all. At least it explains everything. We know why we were really brought here now'.

'That's true, but I still find it hard to believe that I met you, got married and had a baby in just over a year'.

'Well I am irresistible - obviously' said Julie giving a little twirl.

'Don't worry' said Marcus laughing. 'When I send you back, you'll get a chance to do it all over again'.

'And what about all this?' said Zak, gesticulating around. 'Is all this going to happen again? Are we destined to be involved in this time travel project for the rest of our lives? With Ron?'

'Probably not' said Marcus. 'A lot of that will depend on you. I'm going to destroy the time machine when you have gone, but it's not going to stop it from being rebuilt again in your time. It's up to you to discourage me from becoming involved. Find me a new hobby' he said with a grin. 'If all goes as planned, then you shouldn't have to cross paths with Ron ever again'.

'This is too confusing' said Zak. 'Let's just get out of here. I'll try and work it out later'.

'What about the murder charge?' said Julie suddenly. 'If there are no witnesses to the murder, then Zak could still go down for it'.

'You know about that?' said Zak baffled.

Marcus and Julie laughed.

'After I've sent you home, I'll go back and prevent the murder' said Marcus. 'Or prevent Zak from going to the video shop. It shouldn't be a problem'.

They arrived at the control room without incident.

'Where have the guards gone?' said Julie puzzled. 'I thought we would have seen at least one by now'.

'There were four around earlier' said Marcus. 'I shot two when I first arrived, and you put another out of action for a few weeks'. He laughed. 'There may be at least one more somewhere'.

'There could be hundreds' said Zak. 'When we were outside, we had a whole army looking for us'.

'They're probably waiting for orders' said Julie. 'Seems to be how they operate. I haven't seen many around this place since we came in. Perhaps its out of bounds for them'.

'The security tends to be more outside than in' said Marcus. 'No one gets in, so it's not really required inside. I think the four we've seen were only here because of you two. The last one has probably gone and joined the others'.

The door to the control room slid back and they cautiously looked in.

'We're OK' said Zak. 'Let's go'.

Marcus set to work on the computer.

'Who wants to go first?' he said. 'Mum or Dad?' he grinned.

'I can't cope with this?' said Zak. 'You're not helping you know'

'Sorry Dad. You'll have plenty of time to get used to me when you go back'. He looked at Julie. 'Ready to go mumsie?'

She laughed. 'As ready as I'll ever be' she said. 'It's going to be nice to get back to a normal life'.

She went to Zak and put her arms around him, hugging him hard.

'See you back in 1994' she said, giving him a kiss. He kissed her back and smiled.

'I hope it all works out' he said. 'I can't handle all the confusion that time travel causes'.

'You'll be fine' said Marcus. 'Trust me. You will get to live the life that you are supposed to live'.

Julie hugged him too. 'Thanks for everything' she said. 'I don't know what would have happened if you hadn't turned up'.

'I was only helping the family out' he said modestly. 'See you in about nine months. Make sure you look after that baby'. He patted her belly and she laughed.

'I almost forgot. It's going to take a while to get used to the idea'.

A blinding flash made them all jump, and Zak lifted the gun quickly. Two figures lay sprawled in the glass dome, barely moving. Zak walked cautiously over to them, keeping the gun levelled all the time.

The door opened and Ron crawled out, or what Zak could only assume was Ron. His skin had turned a pale grey colour with white patches around the eyes. Most of his hair had fallen out and his ears were streaming blood. He was trying to say something, but the words were coming out raspy and unintelligible, his damaged lungs and throat not able to form them properly. He crawled forward a couple of feet, a look of complete concentration fixed on his pallid face.

Julie let out a cry of disgust and turned away.

Zak and Marcus were looking elsewhere. Behind Ron, still in the dome, was the lifeless form of Randy. He was in much the same state as Ron, but the disease, or whatever it was, had hit him harder. His face was almost completely red as blood had poured from every visible orifice. His nose, mouth, ears and even his eyes had blood dripping from them. There was no hair left on his head at all and there was a bulge protruding from the side of it as if his brain had swollen to twice its size. His fingers were curled right over, almost into a fist, making it seem as if he was ready to fight whatever was attacking him. The thing that made Zak sick the most was the look on the boy's face. Behind the blood, his features were clenched up and frozen in a permanent picture of agony. He hadn't died peacefully.

'Randy?' whispered Marcus, as tears sprung to his eyes. 'Oh my God, Randy. What are you doing here?'

Zak was too stunned to realize that Marcus knew him too. A tear trickled down his face as he remembered the boy who had helped him to escape from Ron's guards, helped him find Julie. He refused to believe that he had been abetting Ron all along.

Marcus went over to him and sat next to him, carefully lifting the boy's head on to his lap and cradling his dead brother. He couldn't tell Zak and Julie. It wouldn't be fair to put them through any more torment. He cried, tears running down his face and dropping onto Randy, mixing with the blood on the boy's face.

Zak turned to Julie who had fallen to her knees and was being violently sick. He walked towards her and put a soothing hand on her back as she retched, gasping to catch her breath. He suddenly spotted Ron.

While everyone was distracted, Ron had set himself a final mission. When he crawled out of the dome, the first thing he saw was Zak holding a gun up to him. The second thing he saw was the laser gun. Marcus had tossed it to the ground earlier in the day and it had slid across the floor and come to rest by a cabinet that housed one of the many computers. It remained there, unnoticed. Until now. Ron knew he was dying, and he focused what strength he had left on getting to that gun. While Zak and Marcus had their attention turned to Randy, and Julie was vomiting, he had painstakingly dragged his limp body across the floor, closing the gap between his outstretched hand and the gun. The pain was excruciating, bits of skin were falling away from his body as it scraped along the ground. The only thing that kept him going was the chance to end things on his terms.

Two feet away.

One foot away.

He stretched forward and his fingers curled around the gun. He had to struggle to lift it, but he had already gone through the pain barrier and a little bit more didn't make a lot of difference.

Just as he lifted the gun, Zak had turned around and spotted him. Ron's eyes were bulging, and a maniacal grin spread across his mouth, showing the bloodied stumps where his teeth used to be. The laser gun was wavering in his hand as he aimed at Zak, but he couldn't hold it steady.

Zak lifted his own gun, but everything started happening in slow motion. He saw the laser come from Ron's gun and creep along the room towards him. It seemed to be going so slowly, and he could clearly see that Ron had missed him. He watched it go past him, heading for Julie, so slowly he could have plucked it out of the air like he'd done with the rabbit yesterday. There's plenty of time, his brain thought. You can push Julie out of the way. He tried, but his feet wouldn't budge because they were moving in slow motion too. He was powerless to stop it.

The laser buried itself in Julie's back and she was pitched forward. She seemed to fall to the ground like a feather, slowly floating down, peacefully even. She'll be OK, thought Zak. It was going too slow for her to be hurt. She'll be fine.

She wasn't. It had all happened in the blink of an eye. Julie was sprawled across the floor, blood coming from the large hole in her back. Ron dropped the gun, all his strength gone and howled. He never meant to hurt Julie. None of this was intended to hurt Julie. He just needed Marcus, or Randy or someone to complete his lifelong work.

Ron's howl was joined by a louder one from Zak, that drowned out the sound of the six shots that came in quick succession from his gun. When the barrel was empty, he kept firing, the clicking sound not registering. He could see every shot hitting Ron. His eyes saw Ron's body being riddled with bullets but none of them seemed to wipe the smile that he was imagining on Ron's face.

Finally, he stopped shooting and walked over to Ron's dead body and picked up the laser gun. That done the trick. The smile disintegrated with the first shot. The other four shots were completely unnecessary.

He slumped to the floor dazed, a blank expression on his face. He didn't know how long he stayed there for, but when he finally got up he realised something.

Randy and Marcus had disappeared.

Chapter 34 – "Zak"

Zak checked Julie once and briefly. He knew she would be dead, and he didn't want to linger over her body. His mind went back to one of the last things that Marcus had said to him.

"You will get to live the life that you are supposed to live"

He knew how to fix it. He knew how to fix everything. He knew a way in which they all could all start over without having anything to do with the time travel project at all.

He went to the computer screen with the map, the coordinates, the destination and began to work on it. He knew exactly where to go. He knew the exact time. He gave a final sad glance at Julie as he left the control room in 2017. If she had been alive, she would have been the only one who saw him leave. No one saw him arrived in 1990.

****

The parking lot was overflowing with cars, but other than that it was deserted. It was funny that he remembered is so well. He had only been here a couple of times and it had been a long time ago. A different life. He could hear the deep, thudding of the music from the party in the distance, and cries of laughter from the people inside enjoying themselves. He dismissed them and set his mind on the task at hand.

There were a lot of cars around him, but he found the one he was looking for very easily. He sat down behind it and waited. He wanted to see her, wanted to hear her voice once more before everything started over.

Time passed. He thought of Julie. He thought of Marcus and Randy. Why had Randy disappeared too? He could guess but he dismissed the train of thought instantly. There was no point dwelling on the past, or the future or whatever it was. A past that he had no recollection of. A future that wasn't going to be his future.

He heard footsteps and then he heard her sweet voice for the first time in years. She was saying the same thing he remembered all those years ago.

'Do you want me to drive darling? You've had a bit more to drink than me'

He heard himself answer.

'No. I'm fine. It's not far. I should be OK'.

'We could get a taxi and come back for the car tomorrow'.

Zak smiled as he sat behind the car listening to the voice of the woman he had loved all those years ago, the woman he had thought of every day. The woman he still loved. If only he had listened to her back then, then all of this wouldn't be happening.

He reached down and put his finger on the valve of the tyre. The air started to come out in a rush. The last thing he heard was Zak opening the door for his wife. As the tyre deflated, he began to fade. It was almost as if he was letting the air out of himself.

'Have a good life Zak' he whispered.

He had gone when Zak walked around to his side of the car.

****

'Shit' exclaimed Zak in disgust.

Mary leaned over and opened the door. 'What's wrong?' she said.

'We've got a bloody flat' said Zak. 'It'll take me ages to swap it over'.

Mary got out and locked the car up. 'Leave it', she said. 'We'll get a cab. I'm not hanging around while you do that'.

'Yes boss' he said dolefully.

Damn! That's all he needed. Tyres weren't cheap. He was about to turn and walk away when he spotted the black cap that covered the valve was on the floor. He picked it up puzzled. How did that get there? He picked it up and screwed it back on. Out of the corner of his eye, he saw that the tyre was nearly worn through in the middle. It made him feel a bit better. It's on its way out anyway, he thought.

He joined Mary, putting a hand around her waist, and leaning in to give her a kiss.

'Let's go and find that cab'.

The End......almost

Chapter 35 – "Julie"

Julie staggered out of the pub with Jenny trying to hold her up.

'Can I drive?' said Julie, tripping down the steps. 'I want to drive. Where's the car?'

'We haven't got a car' said Jenny. 'We got a taxi. Don't you remember?'

'Can I drive the taxi then?'

'No'. Jenny was heading for the phone box outside the pub when a taxi pulled up.

'Are you free?' she called to the driver.

'No luv, I charge like everyone else'.

'I mean. Has anyone booked you?'

He laughed and got out opening the door for them.

'What a gentlemen' said Julie, slurring her words. 'Thank you for your help Mr gentlemen'.

'She's had one too many' said Jenny embarrassed. 'You'll have to ignore her'.

'I'm perfectly fine' said Julie. 'Don't listen to her. Talk to me'.

The cab driver laughed. 'I think your friends right. Let's get you home'.

Julie dozed off in the taxi and was still sleeping when they got to Jenny's house.

'Can you hang on a mo?' said Jenny. 'I'll get the door open and come back for her'.

'I'll give you a hand' said the driver getting out. 'I'll help your friend'.

He opened the door for Jenny, and she ran up the steps as he woke Julie up.

'Come on. Time for bed young lady'.

'Are you going to join me?' said a drunken Julie. 'Jenny wouldn't let me bring someone home with me'.

'Not tonight' said the driver laughing. 'Tell you what. I'll take you out for a drink if you still want to when you're sober'.

'It's a date' said Julie, wagging her finger at him as if to make the point. 'Leave me a name and phone number and I promise to call you'.

The driver reached into the front of the cab and picked up a business card. He scribbled his home phone number on the back.

'Call me at home on this number' he said, handing her the card.

She took it and turned it over, squinting and trying to focus on the name.

'I will Ronald. I'll just have a little sleep first'.

He smiled. 'Call me Ron'.

The End

Authors Note

In the early 1990's, I was working nightshift for a 24-7 computer operations department. The work finished each night at around 2am and we were just machine minding for four or five hours each night. In these early hours of the morning, I taught myself computer programming, we played games, we watched films occasionally, and one day I started to write a book. This book.

The book was completed and saved to a floppy disk (Oh yes....It was that long ago). I printed a copy on perforated computer paper, threw it in a drawer in my bedroom and promptly forgot about it. I never saw myself as a writer and back then, getting a book published wasn't as easy as it is today.

It would be twenty-seven years before it was resurrected. In 2020, I found myself with a month off work due to the world outbreak of the Covid-19 Coronavirus. The floppy disk had long since been lost, but I still had the paper copy of the – then untitled book, which was beginning to fade and curl at the edges.

I started typing up a chapter a day, making minor edits as I went – but the main story and concepts have been left alone. I do often wonder what was going through my twenty-three-year-old brain when I read about water balloons, exploding birds and other mechanical rodents, but I found myself really enjoying the book as I typed it up. I always remembered how it was going to end, but it's amazing what twenty odd years can do to your memory. I'd totally forgotten about Randy and wasn't sure how he fit into the end part of the book until I got there.

I'm sad to say that I forgot to end Humbug's story. Let's hope he was reincarnated and adopted by Ron and Julie in their next life.

I've always found the concept of time travel interesting and totally impossible but love it when a good book or film is written about it. Nothing will ever come close to the brilliance of the Back to the Future trilogy – one of my favourite series of films as I was growing up. I also love a good twist in a book, and I hope that the time travel element was a good surprise for you while reading.

There were some clues though, some little nods to my favourite time travel movies that you may or may not have spotted. If you did, I hope they didn't spoil the twist. If you missed them, well – you're in for a mini Easter-egg treat.

1, The tramp that knocked Zak on the head and stole his money was called Marty. This is a nod to Marty McFly from the "Back to the Future" trilogy. There was also a tramp in back to the Future that saw Marty return from the past.

2, Don Connor who owned the video shop is married to Sarah. Sarah Connor is the main character in the Terminator films (Also one of my favourites) where a robot from the future travels back in time to kill her.

3, Marcus states that he can only get the predicted-future percentage up to 88. Another nod to "Back to the Future". Time travel occurred when the DeLorean reaches 88mph.

4, The funfair sign:-

WELL'S TRAVELLING FUNFAIR

KEEPING YOU ENTERTAINED SINCE 1895

HG Wells wrote the most famous time travel story ever – The Time Machine in 1895.

5, A little more tenuous, but there is a message hidden in Ron's passwords (The book stated that Ron used passwords that meant something to him):-

2126122020 = 21,26,1,2,20,20

421281310 = 4,21,28,13,10

122221320 = 12,2,22,13,20

Take the first letter of each chapter name and substitute above.

Eg, 21 = 'I' (First letter of the name of Chapter 21 is an 'I')

I'll leave you work to this one out.

Jason Diggle May 2020

Printed in Great Britain
by Amazon